I0840697

Voices of the American Revolution

Barry Robbins

Talk+Tell

Title: Voices of the American Revolution

Author: Barry Robbins

Paperback ISBN: 979-8-9910525-9-7

Dedication

To Pam, my caregiver extraordinaire, without whom this work would not have been possible. Words cannot express my gratitude.

Contents

Prelude

D ear Reader,

In your hands, you hold a unique chronicle of the American Revolution. "Voices of the American Revolution" is not a traditional history book, but rather a tapestry of experiences woven from the threads of countless lives touched by the birth of a nation.

The pages that follow contain letters, speeches, journal entries, newspaper articles, and personal reflections that bring to life the transformative years from 1754 to 1789. While these documents capture the essence of real historical events and figures, it is important to note that they are not verbatim transcriptions of primary sources. Instead, they are carefully crafted representations, designed to convey the spirit, emotions, and perspectives of those who lived through these extraordinary times.

The voices you will encounter—from colonial leaders and British generals to common soldiers, merchants, and citizens on both sides of the Atlantic—speak with authenticity, even if the exact words are not those recorded in historical archives.

This approach allows us to explore the human side of history, to feel the hopes, fears, and convictions of those who shaped and were shaped by the American Revolution. It offers a window into the hearts and minds of individuals caught in the transformation from British subjects to American citizens.

As you read, I invite you to immerse yourself in these voices from the past. Let them guide you through the complexities of a conflict that was at once a revolution, a civil war, and the birth of a new nation. Experience these events not just as a series of battles and political decisions, but as a profound human drama that continues to resonate with us today.

May these voices speak to you across the centuries, offering insights into our shared heritage and the enduring dream of liberty that sparked a revolution and created a nation.

Rights of an Englishman

Chapter 1

The Field of Runnymede

Magna Carta, 1215

Warwickshire, England - June 15, 1225

I, Sir Geoffrey of Warwick, set quill to parchment on this, the tenth anniversary of King John's Great Charter. Though my beard now grows grey and my sword arm weakens, the memories of that June day at Runnymede remain as vivid as if it were yesterday.

I close my eyes and I am there again: the green field beside the Thames, the summer air thick with tension and the buzz of insects. Hundreds of nobles gathered, their colorful banners snapping in the breeze. And at the center of it all, King John, his face a mask of barely contained fury.

We had pushed him to this point, we barons. Years of his tyranny, of arbitrary taxes and imprisonment without cause, had driven us to rebellion. "Why should a king be above the law?" my father had asked me the night before. "Are we not all Englishmen?"

I remember the hush that fell over the assembly as Stephen Langton, the Archbishop of Canterbury, began to read the charter. His voice, strong and clear, carried across the field:

"John, by the grace of God King of England, Lord of Ireland, Duke of Normandy and Aquitaine, and Count of Anjou, to his archbishops, bishops, abbots, earls, barons, justices, foresters, sheriffs, stewards, servants, and to all his officials and loyal subjects, Greeting..."

As he continued, I saw the faces around me. Some nodded in satisfaction, others looked skeptical. Could mere words on parchment truly constrain a king?

But what words they were! "No free man shall be seized or imprisoned, or stripped of his rights or possessions, or outlawed or exiled, or deprived of his standing in any way, nor will we proceed with force against him, or send others to do so, except by the lawful judgment of his equals or by the law of the land."

I remember the murmur that ran through the crowd at those words. This was revolutionary—a king agreeing to limits on his power, acknowledging the rights of his subjects.

Of course, John had no intention of honoring the charter. I saw it in his eyes as he sullenly applied his seal to the document. Within months, he would petition the Pope to annul it, plunging us back into civil war.

But something had changed that day at Runnymede. An idea had taken root—that even kings were subject to the law, that we, as Englishmen, had inalienable rights.

In the decade since, through civil war and the reign of young Henry III, the Great Charter has endured. It has been reissued, its protections extended. And with each passing year, it grows not weaker, but stronger in the minds and hearts of Englishmen.

As I sit here in my hall, watching my grandchildren play, I wonder what they will make of this legacy. Will they understand the price paid for the rights we now take for granted? Will they continue to defend these liberties against future tyrants?

I think of my cousins who have sailed to France, of the English merchants I meet in the markets who trade as far as Constantinople. I wonder, how far will the ideas of the Great Charter spread? In a hundred years, or five hundred, will there be men on distant shores who claim these same rights as their birthright as Englishmen?

One thing I know for certain—the words sealed that day at Runnymede will echo through the ages. We are all subject to the law, king and commoner alike. We all have rights that no man, no matter how powerful, can lawfully take from us.

This is the legacy of the Great Charter. This is what it means to be English. And as long as there are those who remember and cherish these ideals, the spirit of Runnymede will live on.

Chapter 2

A Petition for All Englishmen

The Petition of Right, 1628

I, Sir Edward Coke, stand before Parliament, the Petition of Right in my hands. The chamber is silent as I begin to speak.

"My lords, gentlemen, and Your Majesty, I present to you the Petition of Right, a document reaffirming the fundamental liberties of all Englishmen. Let me speak plainly of the rights we seek to protect."

I draw a deep breath and enumerate our demands:

"Firstly, we assert that no tax or loan can be levied without the consent of Parliament. Your Majesty, the forced loans and arbitrary taxes of recent years violate our ancient rights and must cease."

Murmurs of agreement ripple through the chamber. I continue:

"Secondly, we demand an end to imprisonment without cause. No free man should be detained without a writ stating the charges against him. The recent practice of arresting those who refuse to pay unauthorized taxes must end."

I see several members nodding vigorously. These arbitrary imprisonments have touched many families.

"Thirdly, we call for an end to the billeting of soldiers in private homes without the owner's consent. This practice burdens our people and invites abuse."

At this, I notice several of the king's supporters shifting uncomfortably. Good—let them feel the weight of these grievances.

"Fourthly, we insist on an end to the imposition of martial law in peacetime. Civilians must be tried in civil courts, not by military tribunals. The rule of law must prevail in times of peace."

I lock eyes with King Charles, willing him to understand the gravity of these issues.

"Your Majesty, honorable members, these are not new rights we demand, but old liberties reaffirmed. From the Magna Carta to the present day, these principles have been the bedrock of English liberty. We ask only that they be respected and upheld."

As I retake my seat, debate erupts in the chamber. I've laid out our grievances clearly—no taxation without consent, no imprisonment without cause, no forced quartering of soldiers, and no martial law in peacetime. These are the rights of Englishmen, the liberties we seek to protect.

Now it falls to Charles to respond. Will he see the wisdom in reaffirming these ancient rights, or will he set us on a path to conflict? Only time will tell, but whatever comes, we have made our stand for English liberty.

Chapter 3

A New Dawn for English Liberty

The English Bill of Rights, 1689

London, December 16, 1689

My name is Thomas Hawkins, a printer by trade, and I write these words on a day that shall surely echo through history. The air in London is crisp with winter's chill, but there's a warmth of hope spreading through the city's streets.

Just hours ago, I stood among a great crowd outside Westminster, straining to hear as the new Bill of Rights was read aloud. After years of turmoil under James II, it felt as though England herself was taking a deep, cleansing breath.

"No more will we suffer a Catholic monarch," declared the town crier, his voice carrying over the murmurs of the assembled throng. "William and Mary have accepted the crown, bound by law to protect the rights of all Englishmen!"

A cheer went up, and I found myself swept along in the jubilation. But what exactly were these rights we were celebrating? I pressed closer, determined to hear every word.

First and foremost, the Bill declared the absolute right of Parliament to make laws. No longer could a monarch rule by decree or suspend laws at will, as James had done. "Parliament is supreme," the crier announced, "and no King or Queen may overrule it!"

Next came a guarantee that shook me to my core—free elections for Parliament. No more royal interference, no more packed courts to rubber-stamp a monarch's will. We, the people, would choose our representatives freely.

"The right to petition the monarch without fear of reprisals," the crier continued. I thought of the seven bishops James had imprisoned for daring to challenge him. Never again, I hoped.

Then came a proclamation that brought a lump to my throat: "No excessive bail, no cruel and unusual punishments." I remembered my own father, jailed and ruined for failing to pay one of James's arbitrary fines. This Bill of Rights promised an end to such injustices.

"Freedom of speech in Parliament," the crier declared, and I saw several well-dressed gentlemen nearby nodding in approval. Our representatives could now speak their minds without fear of royal retribution.

But it was the next right that caused the crowd around me to erupt in cheers: "The right of Protestant subjects to bear arms for their defense." After years of James's attempts to disarm us, this felt like a restoration of our very manhood.

The crier went on, listing further protections: no standing army in peacetime without Parliament's consent, no taxation without parliamentary approval, no interference in the law through royal prerogative.

As the reading concluded, I stood in awe. This wasn't just a transfer of power—it was a fundamental reshaping of what it meant to be English. The divine right of kings was dead; in its place stood the rule of law, protecting the rights of every Englishman.

Later that evening, as I set type in my shop for tomorrow's broadsheets, I reflected on the day's events. The Bill of Rights wasn't just words on paper—it was a shield against tyranny, a guarantee of liberties my father and grandfather could only have dreamed of.

I carefully arranged the letters: "England Enters a New Age of Liberty." As I worked, I couldn't help but wonder how far these ideas might spread. Would our children and grandchildren understand the magnitude of this day? Would these rights one day be claimed by Englishmen in far-flung colonies across the seas?

Whatever the future might hold, I knew I had witnessed something profound. The Glorious Revolution had given us more than new monarchs—it had given us a new vision of what it meant to be English. A vision of liberty protected by law, of monarchs bound by the will of the people.

As I pulled the first print of tomorrow's news, I felt a surge of pride. This was our legacy, our gift to future generations. The English Bill of Rights—a beacon of liberty in a world too often darkened by tyranny.

Chapter 4

The Seeds of Liberty, 1754

Boston, Massachusetts Bay Colony - May 15, 1754

The afternoon sun slants through the windows of my small schoolroom as I, Jeremiah Quincy, stand before my pupils. Their young faces, some eager, some restless, all turn towards me as I begin today's lesson.

"Young men," I say, my voice carrying to the back of the room, "today we speak of your birthright as Englishmen. For though an ocean separates us from England's shores, we are heirs to a tradition of liberty that spans centuries."

I turn to the chalkboard, writing in large letters: MAGNA CARTA, 1215.

"Who can tell me the significance of this document?" I ask.

Young John Adams, always quick with an answer, raises his hand. "It limited the power of the king, sir. Made him subject to the law, just like everyone else."

"Excellent, John," I nod approvingly. "The Magna Carta established that even the king is not above the law. It protected against unjust imprisonment and excessive fines. These are rights we still claim today."

I write another date: 1628.

"The Petition of Right," I continue. "Building on the Magna Carta, this document further defined the liberties of Englishmen. Who remembers its key points?"

Samuel Quincy, my nephew, speaks up. "It said that the king couldn't collect taxes without Parliament's consent. And that soldiers couldn't be quartered in private homes."

"Very good, Samuel," I say. "It also prohibited imprisoning people without cause and the use of martial law in peacetime. These were crucial protections against royal overreach."

Finally, I write: ENGLISH BILL OF RIGHTS, 1689.

"And this," I say, tapping the board for emphasis, "is the document that shapes our lives even now, here in the colonies. Who can name some of the rights it guarantees?"

The boys call out in turn:

"Free elections!"

"The right to petition the government!"

"No excessive bail or cruel punishments!"

"Freedom of speech in Parliament!"

"All correct," I say, pleased with their recall. "The Bill of Rights also established that no law can be suspended without Parliament's consent, and that no standing army can be maintained in peacetime without parliamentary approval."

I pause, looking around the room. "Do you understand the significance of these documents? They are the foundation of English liberty - your liberty. They protect you from the arbitrary exercise of power, ensure your voice in government, and guarantee your basic freedoms."

Young Josiah Quincy, always the thoughtful one, raises his hand. "But Mr. Quincy, if these are our rights as Englishmen, why do we sometimes hear complaints about the actions of Parliament or the Royal Governor?"

A shrewd question, and one I must answer carefully. "An excellent point, Josiah. While these documents establish our rights, the practical application of those rights can sometimes be... complex. Especially here in the colonies, where we lack direct representation in Parliament."

I can see the boys mulling this over, some frowning in concentration.

"Remember," I continue, "these rights were hard-won over centuries. Our forefathers fought and even died to secure them. It falls to each generation to understand these rights, to cherish them, and when necessary, to defend them."

As the lesson ends and the boys gather their things, I'm struck by the weight of what I've imparted. These lads—the Adams brothers, my Quincy nephews, young Hancock—they are the future of our colony. The seeds of liberty I've planted today may well blossom in ways I can scarcely imagine.

Later, as I walk home along Boston's bustling streets, I overhear snatches of conversation—talk of taxes, of representation, of the rights of colonists. I realize that the discussions we have in my humble schoolroom are echoing throughout the colonies.

We are Englishmen, proud heirs to a tradition of liberty. But we are also becoming something else - Americans. How we reconcile these identities, how we apply the principles of English liberty to our unique situation here in the New World, will shape the future of these colonies.

As the sun sets over Boston Harbor, I find myself wondering what challenges lie ahead. Will the rights we've inherited be enough to secure our liberties? Or will this new land demand new definitions of freedom?

Only time will tell. But one thing is certain—the story of liberty that began with the Magna Carta is far from over. Indeed, here in the colonies, it may just be reaching its most exciting chapter.

French and Indian War

Chapter 5

A Virginian in the Wilderness

Washington's Crucible, May 1754

May 27, 1754 - Night camp in the Ohio Country

The flickering campfire casts long shadows across my makeshift tent as I, George Washington, put quill to paper. Sleep eludes me tonight, my mind awhirl with the weight of tomorrow's decision. The French are near - too near. Their presence in these lands threatens not just the Ohio Company's interests, but the very future of British America.

I finger the rough fabric of my newly-made colonel's uniform. At twenty-two, am I truly ready for this command? The lives of these forty men rest in my inexperienced hands. Their quiet murmurs around the campfires are a constant reminder of my responsibility.

Native scouts brought word of a French encampment not far from here. Diplomacy, they say, is their aim. Yet why come with armed men into disputed territory if not to provoke? The blood of my men, of young Thomas Wagoner, already stains this forest floor from earlier French "diplomacy."

I close my eyes and see again the face of Half-King, our Seneca ally. "Brothers," he said, "the French build forts on land that is not theirs. They bring many men with guns. This is not the way of peace." His people have suffered French duplicity before. Can I afford to be less wary?

A decision must be made. To attack risks war, yet to allow their incursion threatens all we have built here. I think of Mount Vernon and of the fertile Ohio lands waiting to be settled. What future can there be for Virginia, for all the colonies, if we are hemmed in by French interests?

No. We must act. Tonight, under cover of darkness, we will march. We'll approach their camp by dawn, catching them unawares. May Providence guide our path.

The next evening

My hand shakes as I write, the acrid smell of gunpowder still clinging to my clothes. It is done. We attacked at dawn, the element of surprise our ally. The skirmish was brief but deadly. Ten Frenchmen lie dead, including their commander, Jumonville. Twenty-one more are our prisoners.

Victory, yes, but at what cost? This will surely be seen as an act of war. I see the faces of the dead each time I close my eyes—men not so different from my own, their blank stares accusing. Did I choose rightly? Will history judge this day as the necessary defense of British rights, or the impetuous action of a young, untested commander?

I must put aside these doubts. A report must be written, decisions explained, reinforcements requested. The machinery of war is in motion now, and I am caught in its gears.

As I prepare my official account for Governor Dinwiddie, a treacherous thought sneaks in: part of me thrills at this taste of battle, this test of leadership. Is this vanity, ambition, or the hand of destiny?

The Ohio Country has become a crucible, and I feel myself being forged in its fires. What manner of man will emerge, I wonder? Only time will tell.

G. Washington

Chapter 6

The First Shot

Washington's Report on the Jumonville Affair, May 1754

Report to His Excellency, Governor Robert Dinwiddie
From Colonel George Washington
May 29, 1754

Your Excellency,

I write to inform you of recent events in the Ohio Country that may have far-reaching consequences for our colony and His Majesty's interests in the region.

On the morning of May 28th, acting on intelligence from our Seneca allies, I led a detachment of forty men to confront a French force encamped in our territory. We surrounded their position at dawn and, after a brief but intense engagement lasting about fifteen minutes, emerged victorious.

The outcome of the skirmish is as follows:

- Enemy casualties: 10 killed, including their commander, Sieur de Jumonville
- Prisoners taken: 21

- Our losses: 1 killed, 2 wounded

The French party, while claiming to be on a diplomatic mission, was heavily armed and had advanced well into territory claimed by the British Crown. Their true purpose, I believe, was to scout our positions and strength in preparation for further incursions.

This encounter, though small, may well be the spark that ignites a broader conflict. I have no doubt that the French forces at Fort Duquesne will seek retribution. Our current strength is insufficient to withstand a determined French assault.

I urgently request Your Excellency to send reinforcements and supplies. The security of the Ohio Country, vital to the interests of Virginia and the British Empire, hangs in the balance.

Furthermore, I recommend immediate steps be taken to fortify our position. The construction of a proper fort at the Forks of the Ohio is, in my estimation, crucial to maintaining our hold on this region.

I await your further orders and remain your most obedient servant,

George Washington

Chapter 7

The Day the Forest Bled

Braddock's Defeat, July 1755

July 13, 1755

My hands shake as I put quill to paper. Four days have passed since that hellish day near Fort Duquesne, yet I still hear the screams, smell the gunpowder, see the red coats turned redder still with blood. I, Thomas Gist, scout and guide, write this so I might somehow make sense of the senseless.

General Braddock breathed his last this morning. Even now, I see him in my mind's eye as he was when he first arrived—proud, certain, resplendent in his uniform. "Gist," he had said to me, "with British discipline, we'll send these French scurrying back across the sea." God forgive me, but part of me believed him.

I close my eyes, and I'm back on that forest path. The quiet of the morning shattered by that first shot. Then hell itself erupted around us. I've known these woods all my life, but in that moment, the forest became a stranger—menacing, alive with hidden enemies. French and Indian war cries pierced the air, and brave men fell like ninepins around me.

I had tried to warn the General. "Sir," I'd said, "the forest has eyes. We must be cautious." He dismissed me with a wave of his hand. Now those words taste like ashes in my mouth. What good are warnings unheeded?

Young Colonel Washington was a whirlwind that day. I saw him ride by, hat gone, coat torn, but eyes blazing with determination. Unlike Braddock, he understood this war of the woods. I watched him rally men, urge them to take cover, fight as the enemy fought. If more had listened to him, perhaps...but no. It does no good to dwell on what might have been.

The moment I saw Braddock fall is seared into my memory. One moment upright, the next crumpled on the forest floor. As we carried him away, the great general looked so small, so fragile. His last words to me—"Who would have thought it?"—will haunt me till my dying day.

Now, as night falls and the forest grows dark outside my window, I'm left with questions that gnaw at my soul. How did we fail so completely? Over 900 of ours dead or wounded, and for what? The Ohio Valley seems further from our grasp than ever.

Yet, as I sit here, quill in hand, a small spark of hope flutters in my chest. This defeat, bitter as it is, has taught us harsh lessons. The survivors, Washington among them, now understand the true nature of this war. And I've seen a new fire in the eyes of my fellow colonists—a unity born of shared danger.

I do not know what the coming days will bring. The frontier now lies open, and fear grips the settlements. But we are not broken. Bloodied, yes, but not defeated. As for me, I'll return to these woods I call home. They may have betrayed us once, but I know their secrets. And next time—God grant there isn't one—we'll be ready.

The General is dead. May he rest in peace. But we, the living, must go on. These forests, this land—it's ours to lose or to defend. And defend it we shall, whatever the cost.

Chapter 8

The Great Tree of Peace Bends

Mohawk Chief Addresses His People, 1756

Mohawk Valley, 1756

The fire crackled, casting long shadows across the gathered faces of my people. I, Theyanoguin, known to the British as King Hendrick, stood before them. The weight of my years and the gravity of our situation pressed upon me as I began to speak.

"My children, listen well. The world is changing around us, and we must change with it or be swept away. The British and the French, like two great storms, clash above our heads. We cannot stand apart. We must choose."

Murmurs rippled through the crowd. I raised my hand for silence.

"Long ago, the Great Peacemaker brought five warring nations together. He gave us the Great Tree of Peace, its roots spreading to the four corners of the earth, its branches sheltering us all. But now, this tree bends in the wind of war."

I paused, letting the familiar legend settle in their minds.

"The French, they are like a disease that attacks the roots of our Great Tree. They ally with our ancient enemies, the Algonquin and Huron. They seek to choke our hunting grounds, to push us from our lands."

Angry mutters of agreement rose from the gathering.

"The British, for all their faults, offer us the chance to preserve our ways. They promise to respect our lands, to trade fairly. With them, our Great Tree might weather this storm."

A young warrior stood. "But Chief, have the British not also taken our lands? Can we trust their promises?"

I nodded gravely. "Your words carry wisdom, young one. The British have not always been true friends. But consider the beaver."

Curiosity replaced skepticism on many faces.

"The beaver builds his dam, creating a pond where fish flourish. The wolf comes to drink, the eagle to hunt. The beaver did not invite them, yet he benefits from their presence. The pond grows richer, and the beaver's family thrives."

I let the metaphor sink in before continuing.

"We are like the beaver. The British come not because they love us, but because they need us. And in their need, we find our strength. United with them, we can stand against the French and their allies. Divided, we will fall."

I looked out over my people, seeing understanding dawn in their eyes.

"This war is not just about the British and French. It is about our future. If the French win, our lands will be overrun, our people scattered. But if we help the British push them back, we secure our place in this changing world."

"Remember, my children, the Great Tree of Peace was planted not just for the Five Nations, but for all who would follow its laws.

Perhaps, in this alliance, we can teach the British to shelter beneath its branches as well."

As I finished speaking, a hush fell over the gathering. Then, slowly, voices of agreement began to rise. We would join with the British, not as subjects, but as allies. In doing so, we would fight not just for their king, but for our own survival.

That night, as I looked up at the stars our ancestors had followed for countless generations, I prayed to the Great Spirit. May our choice preserve our people through the storm to come. May the Great Tree of Peace stand strong for generations yet unborn.

Chapter 9

A Desperate Gamble

Planning the Assault on Quebec, Sept. 1759

September 10, 1759
Quebec Campaign Headquarters

I, Colonel George Townshend, second-in-command to General James Wolfe, put quill to paper to record the momentous meeting that has just concluded. The fate of our campaign, perhaps of all New France, may well hinge on the audacious plan we have devised this night.

General Wolfe called us together as dusk fell—myself, Brigadier Robert Monckton, and Brigadier James Murray. The air in the tent was thick with tension and the smoke from Wolfe's pipe. Our commander's gaunt face, hollowed by illness and the strain of our thus far fruitless siege, was set with grim determination.

"Gentlemen," Wolfe began, his voice hoarse but unwavering, "we have reached the moment of decision. Winter approaches, and with it, the end of our campaign season. We must take Quebec, or admit defeat."

Murray, ever aggressive, spoke first. "Sir, I say we attack their left flank at Beauport. One decisive blow-"

Wolfe cut him off with a shake of his head. "No, James. We've battered ourselves against their defenses for months. Another frontal assault would be suicide."

I couldn't help but agree. The beaches below Quebec were a killing ground, as we'd learned at Montmorency Falls. But what alternative remained?

It was then that Wolfe unrolled a detailed map of the area west of the city. "Gentlemen, I propose we do what Montcalm believes impossible. We'll scale the cliffs and force battle on the Plains of Abraham."

A stunned silence fell over the tent. I found myself examining the map in disbelief. The cliffs Wolfe proposed to climb were nearly vertical, over 170 feet high.

"Sir," I ventured, "the risks are extreme. If the French detect us-"

"Then we'll be cut to pieces," Wolfe finished for me. "I'm well aware, George. But consider our alternatives. We've tried everything else. This is our last throw of the dice."

As Wolfe outlined his plan, I marveled at its audacity. A diversionary bombardment from our ships and the Levis shore. Small boats to carry the assault force downriver under cover of darkness. And then, the climb.

"There's a narrow path up the cliff face," Wolfe explained, his finger tracing the route on the map. "Barely wide enough for men in single file. But it's our best chance."

Questions flew. How many men? What of supply lines? What if Montcalm refuses battle?

Through it all, I watched Wolfe closely. There was a feverish energy about him, a sense that he was staking everything on this one desperate gamble. And yet, as the details of the plan emerged,

I felt a growing sense of possibility. It was daring, yes, but it might just work.

As the meeting concluded, Wolfe addressed us one final time. "I know I'm asking the near-impossible of our men. But I believe this army capable of great things. Together, we will take Quebec."

Now, as I review my notes and consider the task ahead, I'm filled with a mix of trepidation and anticipation. Tomorrow, we'll set the plan in motion. By the 13th, we'll either stand victorious atop those cliffs or...

No. I mustn't consider the alternative. Quebec will fall. It must.

For King and Country,
Colonel George Townshend

Chapter 10

Scaling Victory

An Account of Quebec's Fall, Sept. 1759

September 13, 1759

My hands tremble as I write this, not from fear, but from the lingering rush of battle. Just hours ago, I, Lieutenant William Ashton of His Majesty's 43rd Regiment of Foot, scaled the cliffs of Quebec in what surely must be one of the most audacious assaults in military history.

Last night, as we silently boarded the boats to cross the St. Lawrence, General Wolfe moved among us. "Remember, lads," he whispered, his gaunt face ghostly in the darkness, "when you reach the top, Quebec reaches its end." A ripple of nervous laughter quickly hushed.

The current was strong, threatening to sweep us past our landing point. In the boat next to ours, I heard the General softly reciting Gray's Elegy. "The paths of glory lead but to the grave," he murmured. I shivered, though the September air was mild.

We landed at the foot of the cliffs just before dawn. Looking up at the sheer face, my heart sank. How could we possibly scale this? But there was no time for doubt. We began to climb, using roots and sparse vegetation as handholds, our boots scrabbling for purchase on the rocky face.

Somehow, we managed to surprise the French picket at the top. In mere moments, the narrow path was secured, and more of our men poured up. As the sun rose, I found myself standing on the Plains of Abraham, scarcely believing we'd made it.

The battle that followed was chaos. The French, caught off guard, rushed to meet us. The crash of musket fire, the acrid smell of gunpowder, the cries of the wounded—all blurred together in a nightmarish haze.

Amidst the smoke and confusion, I saw General Wolfe fall. Even as men rushed to his aid, he waved them off, urging us forward. His last words, as reported to me later, were, "Now, God be praised, I will die in peace."

By day's end, Quebec was ours. Standing on the ramparts, looking out over the mighty St. Lawrence, I was struck by the magnitude of what we'd accomplished. This was more than just a victory—it was the key to North America.

Yet as I write this, my elation is tempered by a sobering thought. We've won Canada, true, but at what cost? And what will this mean for the balance of power in the colonies? As I watch our flag flutter over Quebec, I can't help but wonder what future we've set in motion this day.

Chapter 11

An Empire's Gratitude

Wolfe's Farewell on the Plains of Abraham, Sept. 1759

Quebec, September 14, 1759

The morning mist clung to the Plains of Abraham, shrouding the aftermath of yesterday's momentous battle. I, Captain James Thompson of His Majesty's Royal Engineers, stood among a somber gathering of officers and men. Before us lay the body of General James Wolfe, draped in a British flag, his pale face peaceful in death.

As the senior engineer, I had been tasked with preparing the General's body for its long journey home. The sight of him, so still and silent, was a stark contrast to the dynamic leader who had inspired us all just days ago.

"He looks almost at rest," murmured Colonel Townshend beside me. "Who would have thought yesterday morning that by nightfall, both he and Montcalm would be gone?"

Indeed, the cost of our victory lay heavy on all our hearts. The French general, Montcalm, had also fallen, leaving both armies bereft of their commanders. The irony was not lost on us.

A makeshift altar had been erected, and as the chaplain began the service, I found my mind wandering to the events of the past day. The impossible climb, the desperate battle, the moment of victory snatched from the jaws of defeat—all orchestrated by the man who now lay before us.

"We are gathered here today," the chaplain intoned, "to honor a man who gave his life for King and Country, who with his last breath secured a great victory for the British Empire."

As the service continued, I glanced around at the faces of my fellow officers. Some wept openly, others stood stoic, but all bore the weight of our shared loss and the magnitude of our achievement.

Nearby, I noticed a group of French civilians watching the proceedings. Their expressions were a mix of curiosity, fear, and resignation. One elderly man caught my eye, nodding slightly as if in recognition of the universal nature of grief and sacrifice.

After the chaplain finished, General Monckton, now our commander, stepped forward. "Gentlemen," he began, his voice thick with emotion, "we have won a great victory, but at a terrible cost. General Wolfe's audacity and leadership have delivered Quebec into our hands, changing the course of this war and the future of North America."

He paused, looking out over the misty plains. "But let us not forget the price paid by brave men on both sides. As we prepare to send our beloved general home to England, let us also extend our respects to the fallen of both armies."

A murmur of agreement rippled through the crowd. Even in victory, there was a sense of shared humanity, a recognition of the toll of war.

As the ceremony concluded, I overheard two young lieutenants discussing the future. "What happens now?" one asked. "With Quebec fallen, surely the rest of New France will follow."

"Indeed," replied the other. "But think beyond that. With the French threat removed, how long before our own colonies start to chafe under British rule?"

Their words gave me pause. In our moment of triumph, were we sowing the seeds of future conflict?

As Wolfe's body was carefully placed in a lead-lined coffin for its journey across the Atlantic, I reflected on the general's last quoted words: "Now, God be praised, I will die in peace." He had won his victory, secured his place in history. But for those of us left behind, the work was just beginning.

The flag-draped coffin was carried away, and gradually, the gathered soldiers and officers dispersed. I lingered, looking out over the St. Lawrence River. Quebec stood silent behind us, its future now irrevocably changed.

In that moment, I felt the weight of empire on my shoulders. We had won Canada, yes, but at what cost? And what challenges lay ahead in governing this vast, untamed land?

As I turned to leave, my eyes fell upon a patch of blood-soaked earth where Wolfe had fallen. In that soil, I realized, lay the seeds of a new world. What would grow from them, only time would tell.

Lead Up to Revolution

Chapter 12

A Republic, If You Can Keep It

Franklin and Adams Correspond, 1763

Philadelphia, September 15, 1763

My dear friend John Adams,

I hope this letter finds you well in Boston. I write to you today with news that will surely shape the future of our colonies and, indeed, the entire continent of North America.

The Treaty of Paris has been signed, officially ending our long struggle against the French. On the surface, it appears a great triumph for the British Empire and for us as her subjects. France has ceded all territories east of the Mississippi, save New Orleans, as well as Canada. Spain has traded Florida for Cuba. In short, we are now part of the greatest empire the world has ever seen.

And yet, my friend, I find myself troubled. With the French threat removed, I fear the delicate balance between the colonies and the mother country may soon be upset. Already, there are whispers of new taxes to pay for the war, despite the blood and treasure we colonists have already sacrificed.

But it is the King's Royal Proclamation, just received, that gives me the gravest concern. His Majesty has seen fit to draw a line along the Appalachian Mountains, forbidding settlement beyond it. This land, he decrees, is to be reserved for the Indian nations.

While I have always advocated for fair treatment of the natives, I cannot help but see this as a direct affront to our colonial ambitions and the natural growth of our populations. Many of our citizens fought and died to secure those western lands. How will they react to being told they cannot now settle there?

Moreover, the Proclamation establishes or restructures several new colonies—Quebec, East Florida, West Florida, and Grenada—to be governed directly from London. I fear this is a sign of increased royal intervention in colonial affairs, a trend that may not bode well for the freedoms we have long enjoyed.

John, I must confess that I see storm clouds on the horizon. The very victory that has secured our place in North America may well be the catalyst for a great conflict between the colonies and Parliament. We have grown strong and self-reliant during this war. Will London recognize this, or will they continue to treat us as wayward children in need of guidance and control?

I would value your thoughts on these matters. How are these developments being received in Massachusetts? Do you share my concerns about the future?

Your friend and humble servant,

Benjamin Franklin

Boston, October 3, 1763

My dear Dr. Franklin,

Your letter arrived at a most opportune time, as the news of the Treaty and the King's Proclamation has just reached Boston, causing no small stir among the populace.

I share your concerns about the future of our relationship with the mother country. The restrictions on westward expansion have been met with particular indignation here. Many see it as a betrayal of the sacrifices made during the war.

Your point about the new taxes is especially prescient. There is already talk in London of a Stamp Act to help replenish the British treasury. I fear such measures will be met with fierce resistance here, where we have long enjoyed a degree of fiscal self-determination.

The establishment of new colonies under direct British control is indeed troubling. It suggests a new phase of imperial policy, one that may not look kindly upon the traditions of self-governance we have nurtured over the past century.

You ask how these developments are being received in Massachusetts. I can tell you that there is a growing sense of unease. The joy of victory over the French has quickly given way to apprehension about our future. Many are beginning to question whether our interests truly align with those of Parliament.

In the taverns and meeting houses of Boston, I hear increasingly bold talk. Some even dare to whisper of independence, though such notions seem far-fetched to most. Yet, I cannot help but wonder if the seeds of such radical ideas are not being sown by these very policies we now discuss.

Benjamin, I fear you are right. We stand at a crossroads. The next few years will determine whether we continue as loyal British subjects or forge a new path. Our actions now may well shape the future of not just the colonies, but of the entire continent.

I urge caution, but also preparation. We must be ready to defend our rights as Englishmen, lest we find ourselves reduced to mere subjects of a distant and uncaring Parliament.

Your faithful friend,

John Adams

P.S. Your phrase *"a republic, if you can keep it"* from our last conversation has stuck with me. I wonder if we may see those words tested sooner than we thought.

Chapter 13

Seeds of Discontent

The War's End and a New Beginning, 1763

Philadelphia, October 1763

The tavern was buzzing with conversation as patrons pored over the latest broadsheet announcing the Treaty of Paris and the King's new Proclamation. In a corner booth, four men from different walks of life found themselves drawn into heated discussion.

Thomas Winthrop, a Boston merchant, slapped the paper down on the table. "Well, gentlemen, it seems the war that made Britain master of North America may well be the undoing of that mastery."

William Byrd III, a Virginia planter, nodded grimly. "Damned right. We shed our blood fighting alongside the Redcoats, and now they tell us we can't settle the land we won? It's an outrage!"

James Logan, a grizzled veteran of the Pennsylvania militia, took a long swig of ale before speaking. "Aye, and what of us who already have farms beyond this new line? Are we to be forced from our homes?"

Canasatego, an Iroquois leader invited to Philadelphia for treaty negotiations, listened silently, his face impassive.

Winthrop leaned forward, lowering his voice. "It's not just the Proclamation, my friends. Word from London is they're planning new taxes. They've spent a fortune on this war, and now they expect us to pay for it."

Byrd's face reddened with anger. "We already paid! With our blood and our crops and our trade. I lost good men fighting the French, and now—"

"Now they treat us like we're still children needing mother's protection," Logan finished.

Canasatego finally spoke, his voice quiet but firm. "You speak of land as if it were a coat to be traded. The land is alive. It remembers."

The three colonists fell silent, uncomfortable under the Iroquois leader's steady gaze.

Winthrop cleared his throat. "The issue, Chief Canasatego, is not just land. It's how we're governed. We've grown up, so to speak. This war showed us our strength, but London still sees us as dependent colonies."

Logan nodded. "We fought alongside British regulars. Damn me, but we saved their skins more than once. And now they're sending more troops to 'protect' us?"

"Protection!" Byrd scoffed. "More like they don't trust us. After all we've done!"

Canasatego's eyes narrowed. "You taste now what we have known. The British promise friendship with one hand and take with the other."

An uncomfortable silence fell over the table. Each man was lost in thought, seeing the future through the lens of his own experiences and fears.

Winthrop broke the silence. "Gentlemen, I fear we're standing at a crossroads. This war united us against a common enemy. But now..." He paused, choosing his words carefully. "Now, I wonder if it hasn't shown us that our interests and London's are not as aligned as we once thought."

Byrd leaned back, a look of dawning realization on his face. "By God, Winthrop, you're right. We're not the same colonies that entered this war. We're stronger, more sure of ourselves."

"And less inclined to bow to dictates from across the sea," Logan added.

Canasatego watched the three men, a glimmer of something like pity in his eyes. "You stand where many nations have stood before. Remember this feeling. It may serve you in the days to come."

As the night wore on, the conversation in the tavern grew louder, more heated. The victory over France, so recently celebrated, now felt hollow in the face of new restrictions and looming taxes. The very war that had bound the colonies closer to Britain had also given them a taste of their own strength and a new sense of identity.

In that Philadelphia tavern, as in countless homes and meeting places across the colonies, the seeds of revolution were taking root. The French and Indian War had ended, but a new conflict—one that would reshape the continent—was just beginning.

Chapter 14

The Right to Tax

Debate in the House of Commons, 1764

London, March 5, 1764

The House of Commons buzzed with anticipation. Today's debate on the proposed Sugar Act and the broader question of colonial taxation promised to be contentious. As Members of Parliament took their seats, Prime Minister George Grenville rose to speak.

"Gentlemen," Grenville began, his voice firm, "the question before us today is not merely one of revenue, but of the very nature of our relationship with the colonies. The late war has left our treasury depleted, and it is only right that the colonies, who have benefited greatly from our protection, should contribute to their own defense."

Grenville paused, his gaze sweeping the chamber. "The Sugar Act before us will not only raise much-needed funds but also help regulate trade in our empire. It is our right—nay, our duty—to govern all British domains, including the setting and collection of taxes."

A murmur of agreement rippled through the government benches. But from the opposition came a different response.

William Pitt the Elder, though ill, had insisted on attending. He rose slowly, leaning on his cane. "Mr. Speaker, I must object in the strongest terms to this proposal. While I do not dispute Parliament's right to regulate trade, direct taxation of the colonies without their consent is a dangerous path."

Pitt's words caused a stir. He continued, his voice growing stronger, "The colonists are the sons, not the bastards, of England. As subjects, they are entitled to the inherent rights of Englishmen, including representation in matters of taxation. Taxation without representation is tyranny!"

The chamber erupted in shouts of both approval and derision. The Speaker called for order, and once the noise subsided, Charles Townshend, the newly appointed President of the Board of Trade, stood to speak.

"Mr. Speaker, with all due respect to the right honorable gentleman," Townshend began, nodding toward Pitt, "he fundamentally misunderstands the nature of parliamentary sovereignty. This body has the right and the power to legislate for all British subjects, wherever they may reside."

Townshend's voice rose passionately. "The colonies are our children, and like all children, they must be guided and governed. They enjoy the benefits of British protection and British trade. Is it not right that they should contribute to the cost?"

Isaac Barré, a veteran of the recent war in America, interjected. "And what of the blood they have already spilled in service to the Empire? I have fought alongside these colonists. They are not children, but full-grown men, with a love of liberty as strong as our own."

The debate raged on, with arguments flying back and forth. Some MPs argued that the colonies were already taxed indirectly through trade regulations. Others insisted that more direct measures were needed to assert British authority and raise funds.

As the session neared its end, Grenville rose once more. "Gentlemen, let us be clear. The right of this Parliament to tax the colonies is not in question. It is fundamental to our system of government. The Sugar Act is but the first step in ensuring that all parts of our empire contribute fairly to its maintenance."

He paused, his next words measured. "But let us also remember that with this right comes responsibility. We must govern wisely, always with the best interests of all British subjects in mind."

The vote that followed was largely a foregone conclusion. The Sugar Act would pass, asserting Parliament's right to tax the colonies directly. As the MPs filed out of the chamber, however, the debate was far from over.

In the corridor, Pitt cornered Grenville. "Mark my words," he said, his voice low and intense, "this act will be seen as the first shot in a battle we cannot win. The colonists have grown used to governing themselves. They will not quietly accept direct taxation without a voice in this House."

Grenville shook his head. "You underestimate both our resolve and the colonists' loyalty, William. They are British subjects, and they will accept British law."

As they parted ways, neither man could have fully grasped the momentous consequences of the decision just made. The Sugar Act would indeed prove to be just the first step on a path that would transform the relationship between Britain and its American colonies forever.

In the coming months and years, as news of the act spread to America, the concept of "no taxation without representation" would become a rallying cry for colonial discontent. The seeds of revolution, planted in the aftermath of the French and Indian

War, had just been watered by the very body meant to govern the empire.

The debate in Parliament was over, but the real battle was just beginning.

Chapter 15

The Price of Sweetness

Brewster's Distillery, 1764

Boston, Massachusetts - September 1764

The sweet scent of molasses hung heavy in the air as Joshua Brewster stood in the doorway of his silent distillery. The copper stills, usually gleaming with use, were cold and tarnished. Joshua ran a calloused hand over his face, feeling every one of his fifty-two years.

"Pa?" His son, Thomas, appeared at his elbow. "Mr. Hancock's clerk is here about the molasses shipment."

Joshua nodded wearily. "Send him in, lad."

As Thomas scurried off, Joshua's mind wandered to happier times. He'd inherited this distillery from his father, whose own father had built it with his own hands. For three generations, Brewster rum had been the pride of Boston. Now, thanks to the Sugar Act, it might all come crashing down.

The clerk, a pinched-faced man named Ezra, entered with a ledger tucked under his arm. "Mr. Brewster," he began without preamble, "I'm afraid I have some bad news. The price of molasses has increased again."

Joshua's heart sank. "How much this time, Ezra?"

"Nearly double what it was last month, sir. With the new enforcement measures, smuggling has become too risky. Legal imports are the only option now, and they come at a premium."

Joshua closed his eyes, calculations racing through his mind. At these prices, he'd be losing money on every barrel of rum. "I can't afford this, Ezra. Surely Mr. Hancock understands our situation?"

Ezra's expression softened slightly. "He does, sir. That's why he's offering extended credit to valued customers like yourself. But..." he hesitated.

"But what?"

"But he needs some assurance. Perhaps...a lien on the distillery?"

The words hit Joshua like a physical blow. A lien? On the business his grandfather had built? He felt a surge of anger, not at Ezra or even at Hancock, but at the faceless parliamentarians across the ocean who had so casually upended his world.

"I'll need to think on it," Joshua managed, his voice tight.

After Ezra left, Joshua sank onto a wooden crate, head in his hands. Thomas approached cautiously. "Pa? What are we going to do?"

Joshua looked up at his son, seeing the worry etched on his young face. Thomas was seventeen, the same age Joshua had been when he'd started learning the distiller's art from his father. Now, the legacy he'd hoped to pass on seemed to be slipping away.

"I don't know, son," Joshua admitted. "This Sugar Act...it's not just about the money. It's about how they went about it. No warning, no asking us what we thought. Just...here's a new law, deal with it."

He stood, pacing the length of the silent distillery. "Your grandfather used to say we were lucky, being born British subjects. Said it meant we had rights." He laughed bitterly. "What rights? The right to be taxed without a say? The right to watch our livelihoods crumble for the sake of a war we didn't start?"

Thomas listened, wide-eyed. He'd never heard his father speak like this before.

Joshua continued, his voice rising. "And now these new courts they've set up. No juries, just a judge in the king's pocket. Bill Turner down at the docks? Accused of smuggling. No evidence, mind you, but they convicted him anyway. Took his ship, his cargo, everything."

He turned to Thomas, his eyes blazing. "This isn't right, son. This isn't the England our forefathers came here for. This isn't freedom."

Thomas swallowed hard. "So what do we do?"

Joshua was quiet for a long moment. When he spoke, his voice was low but determined. "We fight back. Not with guns or swords, but with our wits. There's talk of boycotts, of finding ways around these unjust laws. It won't be easy, and it sure as hell won't be safe. But if we don't stand up now, where does it end?"

He placed a hand on Thomas's shoulder. "I wanted to give you a thriving business, son. Instead, I'm afraid I'm giving you a struggle. But it's a worthy one. This isn't just about rum or taxes. It's about what kind of world we want to live in."

As the last light of day faded, casting long shadows through the distillery, father and son stood together, facing an uncertain future. The Sugar Act had done more than raise the price of molasses. It had planted the seeds of rebellion in the hearts of men like Joshua Brewster, men who would rather risk everything than surrender the freedoms they held dear.

The sweet scent of molasses now carried a bitter undertone—the first hints of a revolution brewing.

Chapter 16

If This Be Treason

The Stamp Act, 1765

Williamsburg, Virginia - May 29, 1765

George Washington shifted uncomfortably in his seat in the House of Burgesses. The air was thick with tension and the heat of late spring in Virginia. As he glanced around the chamber, he could see the worry etched on the faces of his fellow burgesses. The Stamp Act, recently passed by Parliament, hung over them like a storm cloud.

Washington's thoughts were interrupted as a slender man with piercing eyes strode to the center of the room. Patrick Henry, the firebrand lawyer from Hanover County, had been a burgess for barely two weeks, but his reputation preceded him.

Henry's voice, initially soft, grew in power as he addressed the assembly. "Gentlemen, I have discovered a mathematical formula of sorts. It is thus: Liberty decreases in direct proportion to the increase of British taxes!"

A murmur ran through the chamber. Washington leaned forward, intrigued. He had always been a man of few words, preferring action to oratory, but he found himself captivated by Henry's passion.

"The Stamp Act," Henry continued, his voice rising, "is not just a tax. It is a dangerous precedent. If we accept this, where will it end? Will they next demand a portion of our crops? The very bread from our tables?"

Several older burgesses shifted uneasily. Speaker John Robinson called out, "Tread carefully, Mr. Henry. Such talk borders on sedition."

But Henry was undeterred. His next words sent a shock through the chamber: "Caesar had his Brutus, Charles the First his Cromwell, and George the Third—"

"Treason!" cried several members, leaping to their feet. Washington felt his heart race. This was dangerous talk indeed.

Henry paused, letting the outcry subside. Then, with a defiant glare, he finished, "—may profit by their example. *If this be treason, make the most of it!*"

The chamber erupted into chaos. Washington watched as burgesses argued heatedly, some supporting Henry, others denouncing him as a traitor. Through it all, Henry stood firm, his resolve seemingly unshakeable.

As the uproar continued, Washington found his mind wandering to his Mount Vernon estate. He thought of the taxes he already paid, of the regulations that hampered colonial trade. Henry's words, inflammatory as they were, struck a chord.

When order was finally restored, Henry presented a series of resolves against the Stamp Act. Washington listened intently as they were read aloud:

"Resolved, that the first adventurers and settlers of His Majesty's colony and dominion of Virginia brought with them and transmitted to their posterity...all the liberties, privileges, franchises, and immunities that have at any time been held, enjoyed, and possessed by the people of Great Britain."

Washington nodded almost imperceptibly. These were not the words of a traitor, but of a man fighting to preserve the rights of Englishmen.

As the debate raged on, Washington found himself torn. His innate conservatism and loyalty to the Crown warred with his growing belief in the colonies' right to self-governance. He had always seen himself as an Englishman, but now, listening to Henry's impassioned arguments, he began to wonder: was he becoming something else? An American, perhaps?

The session stretched late into the evening. In the end, a modified version of Henry's resolves passed by a narrow margin. As Washington left the chamber, the warm night air heavy with the scent of magnolias, he overheard two younger burgesses talking excitedly.

"Did you hear Henry?" one said. ""If this be treason, make the most of it!' By God, that's a man who's not afraid to speak truth to power."

The other nodded fervently. "Mark my words, this is just the beginning. If Parliament doesn't back down, there'll be more than just words flying before long."

Washington walked on, lost in thought. He had always been a man of duty, loyal to the Crown. But now, for the first time, he felt the stirrings of something new—a sense that perhaps his highest duty was not to a king across the ocean, but to his fellow colonists and the land they shared.

As he mounted his horse for the ride back to Mount Vernon, Washington took one last look at the Capitol building. Patrick Henry's words echoed in his mind: "If this be treason, make the most of it!"

Whatever came next, Washington knew that the relationship between the colonies and Great Britain had changed irrevocably. And he, George Washington, planter, burgess, loyal subject of the

Crown, would have to decide where he stood in this brave new world.

Chapter 17

A Taxing Conversation
The Stamp Act, 1765-66

Boston, Massachusetts - April 1766

In the dim light of a lawyer's office, two legal documents lay side by side on a weathered oak desk. One, a land deed from 1764, crinkled its parchment as it turned to its neighbor, a will dated 1765.

"I say," the 1764 deed whispered, its ink slightly faded, "what's that peculiar thing stuck to you?"

The 1765 will rustled indignantly. "It's a stamp, you foolish scrap. Haven't you heard? It's all anyone's been talking about for months."

"A stamp? Whatever for?"

The will sighed, its red wax seal bobbing. "It's a tax, you see. Now every legal document, newspaper, even playing cards must bear one of these stamps. Quite the scandal, I assure you."

The deed's margins crinkled in confusion. "A tax? But I thought only our colonial assemblies could levy taxes."

"Ha!" the will snapped. "Tell that to Parliament. They've decided they can tax us directly, no colonial approval needed. 'Virtual representation,' they call it."

The deed's watermark paled. "But that's...that's..."

"Tyranny?" the will finished. "Many seem to think so. There's been quite an uproar. Riots in Boston, New York, Charleston. I heard a group of gentlemen even held a congress in New York to protest."

"A congress? Colonial representatives meeting without British approval? How daring!"

The will's pages fluttered excitedly. "Oh yes, the Stamp Act Congress, they called it. Representatives from nine colonies, if you can believe it. They drafted petitions to the King and Parliament, demanding the act be repealed. Insisted on 'no taxation without representation.'"

The deed's ink seemed to darken with concern. "And the response from London?"

"Silence, so far. But there's talk of boycotts, of manufacturing our own goods rather than relying on British imports. Some hot-headed fellows are even discussing...independence."

The deed gasped, its fibers stretching in shock. "Surely not! Break away from the Crown? It's unthinkable!"

"Is it?" the will mused. "A year ago, this stamp would have been unthinkable. Who knows what may come if Parliament doesn't relent?"

Just then, the office door creaked open. The documents fell silent as the lawyer entered, a newspaper clutched in his hand. He sat at the desk, his eyes scanning the paper eagerly.

"Well, I'll be damned," he muttered. "They've done it. Parliament's repealed the Stamp Act!"

As the lawyer hurried out to spread the news, the two documents sagged in relief.

"Thank heavens," the deed sighed. "Perhaps now things can return to normal."

The will was quiet for a moment. "Perhaps," it said finally. "But I fear this is only the beginning. The issue was never really about stamps or taxes, you see. It's about power—who wields it and why. That question, my friend, is far from settled."

As night fell over Boston, the two documents lay silent, pondering an uncertain future. The Stamp Act was gone, but the ideas it had awakened—of representation, of rights, of the very relationship between Britain and her colonies—would continue to shape events for years to come.

****

Historical Note:

The Stamp Act, imposed in 1765, was indeed repealed in 1766 due to widespread colonial protest and boycotts. However, Parliament simultaneously passed the Declaratory Act, asserting its right to legislate for the colonies "in all cases whatsoever." This would set the stage for future conflicts, as the fundamental disagreement over Parliamentary authority remained unresolved.

Chapter 18

Liberty's Foot Soldiers
The Sons of Liberty, 1765

Boston, Massachusetts - August 12, 1765

The flickering candlelight casts long shadows as I, Thomas Elderkin, put quill to paper. My hands still shake with excitement from today's events. To think, just three months ago I was but a simple apprentice printer, and now I am a Son of Liberty!

Today's action was not as grand as the Stamp Act protests, but important nonetheless. We plastered the doors of known loyalists with seditious pamphlets, a clear message that the eyes of Liberty are ever watchful. The thrill of sneaking through the darkened streets, heart pounding with every footstep, is one I shan't soon forget.

I still recall the night James Otis recruited me. "Thomas," he said, his eyes afire with passion, "we stand at a crossroads. Will you be a mere subject, or a free man?" How could I refuse such a call?

The inner circle of our group both awes and intimidates me. Samuel Adams, with his fierce intelligence and unwavering conviction. John Hancock, whose wealth and connections provide vital support to our cause. And of course, the fiery Patrick Henry, whose words "Give me liberty or give me death!" still ring in my ears from his last visit to Boston.

Tomorrow, we plan to erect a new Liberty Pole on Boston Common. A symbol of defiance, yes, but also a rallying point for those who cherish freedom. I've been tasked with helping to guard it from loyalists who would surely try to tear it down.

There are whispers of bigger plans afoot. Talk of a unified resistance across all the colonies, of forceful action against British goods and officials. Part of me thrills at the prospect, while another part quakes at the risks. Are we truly ready to challenge the might of the British Empire?

Yet when I think of the Stamp Act, of Parliament's blatant disregard for our rights as Englishmen, my resolve strengthens. We do not act out of mere mischief or rebellion, but out of a deep conviction that our cause is just and necessary.

Samuel Adams often reminds us, "It does not require a majority to prevail, but rather an irate, tireless minority keen to set brush fires in people's minds." We are that minority, and each pamphlet, each Liberty Pole, each act of defiance is a brush fire, slowly awakening our fellow colonists to the cause of liberty.

As I retire for the night, my mind races with possibilities. What will tomorrow bring? Will our actions spark the change we seek, or will they lead to harsh reprisals? Only time will tell. But of one thing I am certain—I, Thomas Elderkin, am proud to call myself a Son of Liberty, and I will do whatever it takes to secure the freedoms that are our natural right as men.

May Providence guide our cause, and may Liberty prevail.

Chapter 19

The Quartering Act Of 1765

THE BOSTON GAZETTE AND COUNTRY JOURNAL

Date: June 3, 1765

PARLIAMENT IMPOSES QUARTERING ACT:
COLONISTS FORCED TO HOUSE BRITISH TROOPS

Boston, Massachusetts Bay Colony—His Majesty's Government in London has enacted a new law that has caused great consternation among the good people of the American colonies. The Quartering Act, passed by Parliament on March 24th and now taking effect in our fair cities, requires colonial assemblies to provide housing and provisions for British soldiers stationed in America.

Under this Act, colonial authorities must furnish barracks and supplies for His Majesty's troops. Should suitable barracks not be available, the Act demands that alternative accommodations be found in alehouses, inns, and livery stables. In the event that such public houses are insufficient, the burden then falls upon private citizens, who may be compelled to open their homes to British soldiers.

The Act stipulates that colonists must provide troops with food, drink, and other necessities, including candles, vinegar, salt, bedding, cooking utensils, and even alcohol. This imposition comes at a time when many colonial households are already struggling under the weight of recent taxation measures.

Governor Francis Bernard, when asked for comment, stated, "This Act is a necessary measure to ensure the proper quartering of His Majesty's forces, who protect our colonies from foreign threats and internal disorder."

However, many colonists view this Act as yet another infringement upon their rights as Englishmen. James Otis, a prominent lawyer and outspoken critic of British policies, decried the Act as "an intolerable intrusion into the sanctity of private homes" and "a violation of the ancient rights of Englishmen."

The New York Assembly, faced with a large contingent of British troops, has thus far refused to comply with the Act's provisions. This defiance has raised concerns about potential retaliation from Parliament.

Some fear that this Act, coming on the heels of the contentious Stamp Act, may further inflame tensions between the colonies and the mother country. Samuel Adams, a leading voice among those critical of Parliament's recent actions, warned, "When our very homes are no longer our own, when we must feed and house those sent to watch over us like children, can we truly call ourselves free men?"

As this Act takes effect, citizens are advised to be prepared for the possibility of being called upon to quarter soldiers. The colonial assemblies continue to debate the appropriate response to this latest directive from Parliament.

This paper shall continue to report on developments regarding the Quartering Act and its implementation in our colony.

-- Joshua Hawkins, Colonial Correspondent

NOTICE: Citizens wishing to voice their opinions on the Quartering Act are encouraged to attend a public meeting to be held at Faneuil Hall on the 10th of June at 2 o'clock in the afternoon.

Chapter 20

A Powder Keg in a Pint Glass, 1767

Boston, Massachusetts - November 15, 1767

Lord help me, but I knew trouble was brewing the moment those lads walked in. I'm Thomas Farrow, keeper of the Green Dragon Inn, and I've seen my share of dust-ups, but nothing like this.

It was a chilly evening, and the tap room was already thick with pipe smoke and the smell of ale. A half-dozen redcoats sat at the bar, as they had every night since being quartered here—not by my choice, mind you. They'd been in their cups since sundown, all loud talk and laughter.

Then in walked young Sam Prescott and his friends, local boys with fire in their eyes and liberty on their tongues. I saw Sam clock the soldiers, his jaw tightening as he led his mates to a corner table.

"Evening, lads," I called out, hoping to keep things civil. "What'll it be?"

"Whatever swill you haven't wasted on those lobsterbacks," Sam shot back, loud enough for the soldiers to hear.

I winced. "Now, Sam, there's no need for—"

But it was too late. One of the soldiers, a burly sergeant, was already on his feet. "What was that, you colonial dog?"

"You heard me," Sam replied, standing to face him. "Or has all that English ale rotted your ears along with your wits?"

I hurried between them, hands raised. "Gentlemen, please. This is a respectable establishment. Let's not—"

The sergeant shoved past me. "Respectable? With vermin like this about?" He spat at Sam's feet.

Sam's friend Isaac lunged forward, but I managed to grab his arm. "Easy now, lad. Think of your mother. What would she say if you came home with a broken nose?"

For a moment, I thought I'd gotten through to him. Then one of the other soldiers piped up: "Aye, run home to mummy, little rebel. Or do you need a redcoat to tuck you in, like the rest of this pathetic colony?"

The room erupted. Fists flew, tables overturned. I ducked a flying tankard, then yelped as a wild punch grazed my ear.

"Stop this madness!" I shouted, trying to separate the brawlers. "You're all Englishmen, for God's sake!"

Sam, nose bleeding, whirled on me. "That's where you're wrong, Mr. Farrow. We're Americans, and it's high time these British bullies learned the difference!"

I groaned, dodging another wild swing. This was more than a tavern brawl—I could feel years of resentment and anger pouring out with every punch.

Desperate, I grabbed my old blunderbuss from behind the bar and fired it into the ceiling. The boom froze everyone in place, plaster dust raining down on their startled faces.

"Right," I panted, lowering the smoking gun. "Now that I have your attention. You lot," I pointed at Sam and his friends, "out the back door. And you," I turned to the soldiers, "back to your quarters. I'll not have bloodshed in my inn."

Grumbling, the two groups separated. As Sam's crew filed out, I heard him mutter, "This isn't over. Not by a long shot."

Looking at the wrecked tap room, I felt a chill that had nothing to do with the November air. Sam was right—this was just the beginning. The Green Dragon had survived countless brawls, but now it felt like we were perched on the edge of something much bigger, much more dangerous.

As I began sweeping up broken glass, I said a quiet prayer. "Lord, grant us the wisdom to step back from this precipice. And if we can't...well, at least let me sell all this ale before the real fighting starts."

Chapter 21

The Price of Tea and Tyranny

The Townshend Act, 1767

Boston, Massachusetts – April 15, 1768

The rhythmic click of knitting needles filled the cozy parlor of Sarah Revere's home. Sarah and her dear friend, Mary Warren, sat by the window, their hands busy with work while their minds grappled with the pressing concerns of the day.

"I tell you, Sarah," Mary said, her brow furrowed as she counted stitches, "I don't know how we're to manage if prices keep rising like this. Have you seen what they're asking for paper at the mercantile? It's highway robbery!"

Sarah nodded, her own knitting momentarily forgotten. "Aye, and it's not just paper. Glass, lead, paints...everything we need to keep a decent home is becoming dear. This Townshend Act is squeezing us dry."

"And tea!" Mary exclaimed. "I nearly fainted when I heard the new price. To think we're paying extra just for the privilege of drinking our own tea."

Sarah's eyes flashed with a mixture of anger and mischief. "Well, my Paul says we ought not to be drinking it at all. He's been attending meetings with Mr. Hancock and the others. They're calling for a boycott of British goods."

"A boycott?" Mary's needles stilled. "But how are we to manage without British imports?"

"We'll have to be clever," Sarah replied, leaning forward. "You know Mrs. Adams down the street? She's organized a spinning bee. Says if we can't buy British cloth, we'll make our own."

Mary looked thoughtful. "I suppose we could. My Thomas brought home some pamphlets about using herbs for tea. Sassafras and the like. Says it's patriotic to drink it instead of English tea."

"Patriotic tea!" Sarah chuckled. "What's next, I wonder? Though I must admit, I do miss a proper cup of Bohea."

The women fell silent for a moment, the gravity of the situation settling over them. It was Mary who spoke next, her voice low. "Sarah, do you think...do you think it will come to war? There's been talk, with the soldiers in the streets and all."

Sarah's hands tightened on her knitting. "I pray it doesn't. But Paul...he says we must be prepared to defend our rights as Englishmen. That these taxes, without our consent, go against everything we hold dear."

"But we're not in England," Mary pointed out. "How can we expect to have a say in Parliament from across the ocean?"

"That's just it," Sarah replied, warming to the topic. "We've governed ourselves for so long. We're loyal to the Crown, of course, but we're also...something else. Something new."

Their conversation was interrupted by a commotion outside. Both women rushed to the window to see a group of British soldiers marching down the street, their red coats a stark contrast to the dusty road.

"More troops," Mary whispered. "They say it's to help collect the taxes and keep order. But it feels..."

"Like an occupation," Sarah finished grimly.

As they returned to their seats, Mary sighed heavily. "What's to become of us, Sarah? Of our children? Sometimes I fear for the future."

Sarah reached out and squeezed her friend's hand. "We'll endure, Mary. We always have. And who knows? Perhaps all this trouble will lead to something better. A new way of doing things."

The women returned to their knitting, the gentle click of needles resuming. But the air was charged with a new energy—a mixture of anxiety and determination. As they worked, they continued to talk, of rising prices and creative economies, of political meetings and whispered dissent.

And though neither of them could have imagined it then, their simple act of adapting to these harsh economic realities was its own form of revolution. In kitchens and parlors across the colonies, women like Sarah and Mary were not just witnessing history—they were helping to shape it, one difficult decision at a time.

As the afternoon wore on, the talk turned to more immediate concerns—children's lessons, upcoming social events, the latest town gossip. But underlying it all was a new sense of purpose, a growing awareness that their daily choices were part of something larger, something that might just change the world.

Chapter 22

News from Across the Sea, 1768

London, England - August 12, 1768

The Ashton family gathered in their comfortable London sitting room, eagerly awaiting the reading of the latest letter from their cousins in Boston. Thomas Ashton, a prosperous merchant, broke the seal on the letter as his wife Margaret and their children, Edward and Jane, leaned in close.

"It's from Cousin William," Thomas announced, adjusting his spectacles. "Dated July 1st, 1768. My dear family," he began reading aloud:

"I hope this letter finds you well. Life in Boston grows more tumultuous with each passing day. The Townshend Acts have thrown our city into turmoil. You've likely heard of these new taxes on glass, paper, lead, paint, and tea, but I wonder if you truly understand their impact on our daily lives.

"Just last week, I witnessed a crowd of angry colonists parading an effigy of Charles Townshend through the streets. The atmosphere here is one of barely contained rage. Many of our neighbors have signed a non-importation agreement, vowing to boycott British goods until these unjust taxes are repealed.

"Margaret, you asked in your last letter about the availability of your favorite tea. I'm afraid I must disappoint you. Many here now view the drinking of tea as an unpatriotic act. Liberty tea, made from local herbs, is becoming quite popular as a substitute."

Margaret clicked her tongue disapprovingly. "How absurd! Surely they can't blame the tea itself?"

Thomas continued reading: "You may have also heard rumors of British troops being sent to Boston. I can confirm these are true. The sight of red-coated soldiers in our streets has only inflamed tensions further. Many here fear we are one spark away from open conflict."

Young Edward's eyes widened. "Are they going to war, Father?"

Thomas paused, considering his words carefully. "I'm sure it won't come to that, son. Surely, once Parliament understands the colonists' concerns, a compromise will be reached."

He returned to the letter: "Thomas, I know you've always been a staunch supporter of Parliament, but I implore you to consider our position. We are not seeking charity or special treatment. We ask only for the rights guaranteed to us as Englishmen—to have a say in the laws that govern us, to not be taxed without our consent.

"Jane, you asked about life for young ladies in the colonies. I'm afraid even they have been caught up in our political strife. Many have taken to spinning their own cloth rather than buying British textiles. They call themselves 'Daughters of Liberty.'"

Jane gasped, a mix of shock and admiration on her face. "How exciting! Though I can't imagine giving up my fine English dresses."

Thomas's brow furrowed as he read the next part: "I must confess, dear family, that I find myself torn. I have always considered myself a loyal subject of the Crown. Yet with each new proclamation from Parliament, I feel my allegiance strained. We are proud of our English heritage, but we are also becoming something new here in the colonies—dare I say, Americans?"

The family sat in stunned silence for a moment. It was Margaret who finally spoke. "Surely William exaggerates. After all, are they not enjoying the protection of the British Empire? Is it not right they should contribute to its upkeep?"

Thomas sighed heavily. "Perhaps. But I can't help but wonder if we in London truly understand their grievances. William has always been level-headed. If he speaks of such discontent, the situation must be grave indeed."

He finished reading the letter, which closed with personal news and warm wishes. As Thomas folded the paper, the family sat lost in thought, the comfortable familiarity of their sitting room suddenly feeling very far removed from the turmoil across the Atlantic.

"Father," Edward asked, breaking the silence, "are Cousin William and the others still British? Or are they becoming something else?"

Thomas stared out the window at the busy London street beyond. "I don't know, son. I truly don't know. But I fear we may all soon have to decide where our loyalties lie—with Parliament or with our kin across the sea."

As the summer evening deepened outside, the Ashton family continued to discuss the letter, their conversation a mix of concern, confusion, and curiosity about the growing divide between Britain and its American colonies. Little did they know that the events unfolding across the Atlantic would soon reshape not just their family, but the entire world.

Chapter 23
Fit to Print, 1768

London, England - September 3, 1768

Edward Whitby, editor of the London Chronicle, stared at the stack of reports on his desk, his brow furrowed in concentration. The flickering candlelight cast long shadows across the cluttered office as the sounds of the printing press clattered from the floor below.

"Blasted colonies," he muttered, reaching for his quill. "Can't they simply pay their taxes like the rest of us?"

As he began to draft the next day's leading article, Whitby reflected on the challenge before him. How to report on events happening an ocean away? How to balance the official government line with the troubling reports trickling in from merchants and personal correspondence?

He glanced at the official dispatch from the Colonial Office:

"His Majesty's Government reaffirms its right to govern all British territories. The deployment of troops to Boston is a precautionary measure to ensure the safety of loyal subjects and the enforcement of lawful taxes."

Whitby snorted. Precautionary measure indeed. The reports from his sources in Boston painted a far different picture.

He picked up a letter from James Coburn, a merchant with extensive ties to New England:

"The situation in Boston grows more volatile by the day. The customs officials are virtual prisoners in their own homes, fearing attack from mobs opposed to the Townshend Acts. There is talk of boycotts against all British goods. If this continues, many of us will face ruin."

Whitby sighed, dipping his quill in ink. He began to write:

"Unrest Continues in American Colonies"

He paused, considering his next words carefully. To report the full extent of the colonists' grievances might be seen as seditious. Yet to parrot the government line entirely would be a disservice to his readers.

"Recent reports from Boston suggest growing tensions between colonial subjects and representatives of His Majesty's Government. The implementation of the Townshend Acts has met with some resistance..."

Whitby leaned back, dissatisfied. "Some resistance." The words felt weak, inadequate to describe the turmoil his sources reported. But how much could he safely say?

He thought of his readers—the merchants worried about their investments, the politicians debating colonial policy, the ordinary Londoners trying to make sense of events in far-off lands. They deserved the truth, or at least as much of it as he could provide.

With renewed determination, Whitby crossed out his opening lines and began again:

"Boston Teeters on the Brink of Open Rebellion"

"Sources close to events in the Massachusetts Bay Colony report a state of near-revolt in response to recently imposed taxes. While His Majesty's Government maintains these measures are both lawful and necessary, colonial leaders argue they violate long-standing rights of British subjects."

Whitby paused, considering the potential repercussions of such bold language. But the role of the press, he reminded himself, was to inform, not merely to appease.

He continued writing, carefully balancing official statements with reports from his colonial sources. He detailed the boycotts, the protests, the growing tension between troops and citizens on Boston's streets.

As he neared the end of his article, Whitby felt compelled to offer some context for his British readers:

"While it is easy to dismiss these colonial protests as mere rabble-rousing, this publication urges readers to consider the broader implications. The questions raised by our American brethren strike at the heart of what it means to be British. Are the rights guaranteed by our ancient laws and customs applicable to all subjects of the Crown, regardless of their distance from London? And if not, can we truly claim to be a nation governed by law rather than mere expediency?"

Whitby sat back, reading over his work. It was a risk, to be sure. There would likely be angry letters from government officials, perhaps even accusations of disloyalty. But it was, he believed, as fair and honest an account as he could give.

As he handed the article to his typesetter, Whitby felt a mixture of pride and apprehension. In these turbulent times, the role of a free press was more important than ever. He only hoped his readers—and the government—would agree.

"The truth, as best we can discern it," he murmured to himself. "Let the consequences fall where they may."

With that, Edward Whitby, editor of the London Chronicle, stepped out into the foggy London night, leaving his words to make their way into the minds and conversations of a nation grappling with the growing crisis in its American colonies.

Chapter 24

Blood on King Street

The Boston Massacre, March 1770

Boston, March 5, 1770

My hands shake as I put quill to paper, the events of this evening etched into my mind with terrible clarity. I, Rebecca Sprague, a seamstress of twenty-four years, write this account lest I wake tomorrow and find it all a dreadful dream.

The air was crisp with winter's lingering chill as I made my way home from Mistress Lamb's shop. King Street was alive with the usual bustle of evening, though there was an undercurrent of tension I'd grown accustomed to these past months. The red-coated soldiers standing guard at the Custom House were a constant reminder of our strained circumstances.

I noticed a group of young apprentices gathered near the sentry, their voices raised in mockery. "Lobster backs!" one called out, and I recognized young Christopher Monk, the son of our neighbor. I made to hurry past, not wanting any part of the trouble brewing.

But then I saw Samuel Gray, a rope maker I knew from church. He approached the group, his face serious. "Come away, lads," he called to them. "No good will come of this."

Before the boys could respond, a commotion erupted further down the street. More colonists were gathering, their angry shouts filling the air. To my horror, I saw some of them carrying sticks and throwing snowballs at the soldiers.

The sentry, looking frightened, called for reinforcements. Within moments, more redcoats arrived, led by a young officer. They formed a semicircle, their muskets at the ready.

"Surely they won't fire," I thought. "Not into a crowd of unarmed citizens."

The mob pressed closer. I saw Samuel Gray step forward, his hands raised as if to calm the situation. Then, without warning, a shot rang out.

Time seemed to slow. I watched in disbelief as Samuel stumbled backward, a bloom of red spreading across his chest. He fell, his eyes wide with shock.

More shots followed. The crowd scattered in panic, but some brave souls rushed to help the fallen. I stood frozen, unable to move, unable to comprehend the horror unfolding before me.

When the smoke cleared, five men lay on the ground. With a jolt of recognition, I saw young Christopher Monk among them, writhing in pain. And there, motionless on the bloodstained snow, lay Crispus Attucks, a sailor I'd often seen at the docks.

The soldiers looked as shocked as we were, staring at their smoking muskets as if they couldn't believe what had happened. Their young officer was shouting, trying to restore order.

I found myself moving, driven by some instinct to help. I knelt beside Christopher, tearing a strip from my petticoat to press against his wound. "Hold on, lad," I whispered, my voice sounding strange to my own ears.

The next hours passed in a blur. More soldiers arrived, pushing back the crowd. I heard someone say that Governor Hutchinson had been summoned. There was talk of arrest, of murder, of retribution.

As I sit here now, in the quiet of my room, I can scarcely believe what I've witnessed. Five men shot down on King Street, their blood staining the snow. Good men, men I knew, whose only crime was to stand up to what they saw as injustice.

I fear for what this night will bring. Already, I hear the murmur of angry voices in the streets. The resentment that has been building these past years has found its spark. What inferno might now engulf us?

And yet, amidst my horror and outrage, I find myself trembling with a different emotion - fear. Fear of what this means for our city, for our colony. Fear of the retribution that may come, from both sides.

As I prepare for a sleepless night, one thought echoes in my mind: nothing will ever be the same again. The shots fired on King Street this evening may well be the ones that set our world ablaze.

May God have mercy on us all.

Chapter 25

A Redcoat's Lament

The Boston Massacre, March 1770

Boston, March 7, 1770

I, Private Thomas Preston of His Majesty's 29th Regiment of Foot, set down these words with a heavy heart and troubled mind. The events of two nights past weigh upon me, as does the knowledge that I may soon stand trial for my actions.

It was a night like many others of late—tense, cold, with an air of hostility that made every shadow seem a threat. We'd been stationed in Boston for months, facing daily taunts and provocations from the townspeople. "Lobster backs," they called us, among cruder epithets. We were soldiers, trained for battle, not constables meant to keep the peace in a hostile town.

That fateful evening, I was on duty near the Custom House when I heard the alarm - "Help, soldiers!" It was Private White, the sentry, calling for assistance. A mob had gathered, hurling not just insults but ice, stones, and clubs.

I led a group of seven men to the scene. The crowd before us was a seething mass of anger, scores of colonists armed with clubs and cutlasses. They pressed in, daring us to fire, pelting us with missiles. "Fire!" they shouted, "You dare not fire!"

We formed a semicircle, bayonets fixed. I ordered the men not to fire—we were soldiers, not murderers. But the mob grew bolder, striking at us with clubs, pressing ever closer.

Then came a moment I'll never forget. A club flew from the crowd, striking Private White. He fell, then rose, his musket raised. I shouted, "Hold your fire!" But in that instant, a shot rang out.

God help me, I don't know who fired first. The noise, the confusion—it was chaos. More shots followed. When the smoke cleared, five colonists lay on the ground, dead or dying.

The horror of that moment is seared into my memory. This was not what I had enlisted for. We are soldiers of the Crown, sworn to protect, not to slaughter civilians in the street.

Now, as I await whatever justice this colony deems fit to dispense, I find myself torn. We acted to defend ourselves, of that I'm certain. The mob was violent, the threat real. And yet, the sight of those men lying in the snow, their blood staining the white drifts red—it haunts me.

I think of the young lad, barely more than a boy, who was among the fallen. What was he doing there? What fervor drove him to stand against armed soldiers? And what will become of his family, now bereft of a son?

There's talk that John Adams, a prominent lawyer and no friend to the Crown, may defend us at trial. It's a strange twist in this already bizarre tale. Will he see that we were men in an impossible situation, or paint us as bloodthirsty tyrants?

I joined the army to serve King and country, to be part of something greater than myself. Never did I imagine I'd find myself at the center of what may become a turning point in history.

As I write these words, I hear angry voices in the streets below. The people of Boston cry for blood - our blood. The irony is not lost on me. We are reviled for killing, and they would kill us in turn. Where does this cycle of violence end?

Whatever comes, I will face it as a soldier should—with courage and honor. But I pray that someday, when tempers have cooled and reason prevails, both sides will see the tragedy of that night for what it was—a moment when fear and anger overtook humanity, with devastating consequences.

May God grant us all the wisdom to find a path forward from this dark moment. And may He forgive us for the blood spilled on King Street, for I fear the stain of it will mark us all for years to come.

Chapter 26

A Mother's Grief

The Boston Massacre, March 1770

Boston, March 6, 1770

My dearest Samuel,

The quill feels heavy in my hand as I write these words you'll never read. The sun rose this morning on a world without you in it, and I find I barely recognize it.

Just yesterday, you were here, my beautiful boy of seventeen summers. Your laughter echoed through our home, your dreams as bright as the future I imagined for you. Now, all that remains is a terrible silence and the crushing weight of a mother's grief.

They tell me you were brave, my Samuel. That when the soldiers opened fire on King Street, you rushed to help the fallen. Of course you did. That was your nature—always thinking of others, always ready to lend a hand. Even as a small child, you'd bring home injured birds and stray kittens, determined to heal them.

I close my eyes and see you as you were just yesterday morning. You sat at the breakfast table, talking excitedly about your apprenticeship, about the life you were going to build. "I'll make you proud, Ma," you said, your eyes shining. Oh, my darling boy, you already had. Every day of your life, you made me proud.

They brought you home late last night, carried by your friends, your body broken by a soldier's bullet. I kept vigil by your bedside, praying for a miracle I knew wouldn't come. I held your hand as you slipped away, whispering how much I loved you, how proud I was of the man you'd become.

This morning, I washed and dressed your body for burial. My hands shook as I smoothed your hair, as I straightened the collar of your best shirt. How many times had I done this when you were alive, sending you off to church or to your apprenticeship? But this time, you didn't squirm or protest. This time, you were so terribly still.

The house is full of people now—neighbors, friends, fellow parishioners. They bring food I cannot eat, offer condolences I can scarcely hear. Their faces are a blend of sorrow and anger. There's talk of retribution, of justice. But what justice can there be for a mother who's lost her child?

I overhear them speaking of you as a martyr, a symbol of our colony's struggle against tyranny. They say your death will not be in vain, that it will rally others to the cause. But to me, you're not a symbol. You're my Samuel, my little boy who was afraid of thunderstorms, who loved apple pie, who dreamed of one day sailing to distant lands.

As the day wears on, my grief gives way to questions that gnaw at my soul. Why were you there on King Street? What drove you to stand against armed men? Did you know the danger, or did you think, in your youthful innocence, that justice would prevail without bloodshed?

And what of the soldier who fired the shot that took you from me? Does he know your name? Does he understand what he's done—not just to you, but to all who loved you? Does he have a mother who, like me, sent him out into the world with hope and pride?

The sun is setting now, casting long shadows across your empty room. Tomorrow, we'll lay you to rest in the cold March ground. How am I to bear it, Samuel? How am I to go on in a world that no longer holds you?

They say time heals all wounds, but I cannot imagine a day when the pain of losing you will lessen. You were my heart, my joy, my hope for the future. With you gone, a part of me has died too.

Yet even in my anguish, I hear your voice urging me to be strong, to live the life you no longer can. I will try, my darling boy. For you, I will try.

Sleep well, my Samuel. Know that you are loved, that you will always be loved. And though we are parted now, I hold to the hope that one day, in God's good time, we will be together again.

Until then, my precious child, until then.

Your loving mother,

Elizabeth Maverick

Chapter 27

A View from London

London, England - April 12, 1771

My dear Cousin William,

I pray this letter finds you and your family in good health and spirits. It has been some time since we last corresponded, and I fear recent events compel me to put quill to paper.

News has reached London of a most disturbing incident in Boston. The papers here call it a "massacre," though official reports paint a different picture. It is said that on the night of March 5th last year, a mob of colonists attacked a group of British soldiers, pelting them with stones and sticks. The soldiers, fearing for their lives, fired into the crowd, killing five and wounding several others.

William, I confess I am deeply troubled by these events. The death of any of His Majesty's subjects is a tragedy, but I find myself wondering how matters in Boston have deteriorated to such a state. Are conditions truly so dire that common folk would attack the very soldiers sent to protect them?

The mood here in London is one of shock and confusion. Many question why troops were necessary in Boston at all, while others argue their presence was clearly justified given the colonists' behavior. There is much debate in the coffee houses and taverns about the true nature of these "Sons of Liberty" we hear so much about. Are they principled patriots as some claim, or merely rabble-rousers stirring up trouble?

I must admit, William, that I find myself torn. You know I have always been a staunch supporter of Parliament and the Crown. Yet I cannot help but wonder if there is more to this situation than we are being told. Your letters have hinted at growing discontent, but I confess I did not fully grasp the depth of feeling until now.

Margaret asks me to inquire about your family's safety. Are you far from these disturbances? How do you and Mary explain these events to the children? Young Edward, in particular, has been most curious about his American cousins and the stories he hears.

I feel I must also address the rumors circulating here about a growing movement for "independence" in the colonies. Surely, this is an exaggeration? While I understand there are grievances to be addressed, I cannot fathom that loyal British subjects would consider severing ties with the mother country. Please, cousin, tell me plainly—is there any truth to these whispers?

Know that despite the distance between us, you and your family are often in our thoughts. These are troubling times, but I have faith that cooler heads will prevail. Surely, there is more that unites us as Britons than divides us?

I eagerly await your reply and any insights you can provide into the true state of affairs in Boston and beyond. May God grant us all the wisdom to find a peaceful resolution to these troubles.

Your affectionate cousin,

Thomas Ashton

P.S. Jane asks me to inquire whether you've had any success
in procuring more of that delightful colonial tea she so enjoyed.
Though I fear, given current sentiments, that might be a rather
sensitive topic. Perhaps it's best we stick to coffee for the time
being!

Chapter 28

The Pen is Mightier

Committees of Correspondence, 1772

Boston, Massachusetts - November 2, 1772

Samuel Adams hunched over his desk, the flickering candle-light casting long shadows across the room. Outside, the streets of Boston were quiet, but within the confines of his modest home, a revolution was brewing.

He dipped his quill in ink and began to write:

"To the Town of Lexington,

Gentlemen,

The dark clouds of tyranny, which have long threatened these colonies, grow ever more ominous. We in Boston have suffered grievously under the heavy hand of Parliament and their so-called Townshend Acts. But we are not alone in our suffering, nor should we be alone in our resistance."

Adams paused, considering his next words carefully. The idea had come to him weeks ago, during a heated discussion at the Green Dragon Tavern. If only there were a way to unite the colonies, to share information and coordinate their efforts...

He resumed writing:

"It is with this in mind that we, the citizens of Boston, have established a Committee of Correspondence. Our aim is simple yet profound: to create a network of communication among all the towns of Massachusetts, and God willing, among all thirteen colonies."

A smile played at the corners of Adams' mouth. Let the British try to control a people united in purpose and informed of their rights.

"We propose that each town establish its own committee, tasked with corresponding regularly with others throughout the colony. Through this network, we may share news of British transgressions, coordinate our responses, and stand united in defense of our liberties."

As he wrote, Adams' mind raced with the possibilities. No longer would Boston stand alone against British tyranny. No longer would news of protests and boycotts be confined to a single town or colony.

"To begin this great work, we ask that you consider the following questions:

1. Do not the people of Massachusetts have a right to petition the King?

2. Is not the levying of taxes upon us without our consent a violation of our natural and charter rights?

3. Has not the sending of armed troops to enforce unjust laws proven fatal to the peace and liberty of this colony?"

Adams knew these questions would spark fierce debate in town meetings across Massachusetts. But debate was exactly what was needed. The people needed to be engaged, to understand the gravity of their situation.

"We eagerly await your responses and your commitment to join us in this endeavor. Let us show the world that though we may be separated by distance, we are united in our love of liberty and our determination to secure our rights as freeborn Englishmen."

As he signed the letter, Adams felt a surge of hope. This was more than just a committee; it was the beginning of a new kind of revolution. Not one fought with muskets and cannons, but with words and ideas.

He sealed the letter and set it aside, ready to be copied and sent to every town in Massachusetts. Then he began another, this one addressed to the colony of Virginia. If this idea took root, it could spread like wildfire through all the colonies.

As the first light of dawn crept through his window, Samuel Adams finally set down his quill. He had not slept, but he was more invigorated than ever. The Committees of Correspondence would be the invisible threads binding the colonies together, creating a tapestry of resistance that the British could neither see nor easily unravel.

"The pen is indeed mightier than the sword," Adams murmured to himself as he finally sought his bed. "And we shall wield it with all the skill and determination we possess."

Little did he know that the network he was creating would become the nervous system of a revolution, transmitting the ideas of liberty and self-governance across a continent poised on the brink of transformative change.

Chapter 29

The Weight of Words

Committees of Correspondence, 1773

Richmond, Virginia - July 15, 1773

The summer sun beat down mercilessly as I, James Hawkins, mounted my horse outside the nondescript tavern on the outskirts of Richmond. My heart raced, not from the heat, but from the gravity of the task I had just been entrusted with.

Mere moments ago, I had stood in the presence of greatness. Patrick Henry, his eyes blazing with the same fire I'd seen when he spoke against the Stamp Act, had pressed a sealed packet into my hands. Beside him, Thomas Jefferson nodded solemnly.

"James," Henry had said, his voice low and urgent, "what we give you now is not merely paper and ink. It is the lifeblood of liberty. Guard it with your life."

Jefferson added, "Remember, lad, you carry the hopes of Virginia, and perhaps all the colonies, with you. Trust no one. Speak to no one of your task."

Now, as I urged my horse forward, their words echoed in my mind. At nineteen, I had thought myself a man grown. But in that tavern room, faced with the trust these great men placed in me, I felt like a child again.

The packet, safely tucked inside my jacket, seemed to burn against my chest. Its contents were unknown to me, but I could guess. News, plans, perhaps even calls to action for our brethren in Maryland, Pennsylvania, and beyond. I was a link in a great chain, the Committees of Correspondence binding the colonies together in common cause.

As Richmond faded behind me, the enormity of my task began to sink in. I was no longer just James Hawkins, son of a shopkeeper. I was a courier for the cause of liberty. Each hoofbeat took me further from home and deeper into a world of intrigue and revolution.

The road stretched before me, long and fraught with danger. British patrols, loyalist spies, even common thieves—any could spell disaster for my mission. Yet the fear that fluttered in my stomach was overwhelmed by a surge of pride. I, James Hawkins, had been chosen for this task. Me, deemed worthy to play a part in this grand struggle for our rights as Englishmen.

As the day wore on, I passed other travelers on the road. A group of farmers nodded respectfully, tipping their hats. Did they know? Could they sense the importance of my journey? I straightened in my saddle, feeling ten feet tall.

"Good day, young sir," called an elderly man leading a laden mule. "What brings you to the road this fine day?"

I nearly burst with the desire to tell him, to shout to the world the importance of my task. But Henry's words rang in my ears. "Trust no one."

"Just delivering some letters for my father's business," I replied, the lie tasting bitter on my tongue.

As I rode on, I thought of all I had heard in recent months. The tea tax, the growing unrest in Boston, whispers of resistance spreading through the colonies like wildfire. And now, I was part of it all. A small part, perhaps, but a part nonetheless.

Night was falling as I approached a crossroads. To the left, safety and comfort at a well-known inn. To the right, a harder road but one that would shave hours off my journey. I thought of the packet against my chest, of Patrick Henry's burning eyes, of the cause that was so much bigger than my own comfort.

I turned right.

As the stars began to twinkle overhead, I allowed myself a small smile. Tomorrow, I would deliver my precious cargo. The words I carried would be read, discussed, acted upon. And though my name would never appear in any history book, I would know. I, James Hawkins, had played my part in the great events unfolding across the colonies.

The weight of the packet was heavy, but I bore it gladly. For it was not just paper and ink I carried, but the very future of a nation yet to be born.

Chapter 30

A Brew of Rebellion

The Boston Tea Party, Dec. 1773

Boston Harbor, December 16, 1773

John Hawkins, Son of Liberty

My heart pounded as I adjusted my makeshift Mohawk headdress. The night air was crisp, filled with tension and possibility. Weeks of heated debates in taverns and secret meetings had led to this moment.

"Ready, John?" Samuel Adams clasped my shoulder, his eyes gleaming with purpose.

I nodded, trying to steady my nerves. We were about to strike a blow against British tyranny, to show King George he couldn't force his taxes down our throats. As our group of "Mohawks" moved towards Griffin's Wharf, I couldn't help but feel the weight of history upon us.

William Chambers, British Tea Merchant

I paced the deck of the Dartmouth, unease gnawing at my gut. Three weeks we'd been stuck in this blasted harbor, our cargo of tea untouched. The colonists' refusal to allow the tea to be unloaded was maddening enough, but the growing crowds on the shore boded ill.

"Mr. Chambers," Captain Hall approached, his face grim. "There's talk in town of action tonight. I fear for the safety of our ship and cargo."

I nodded, gazing at the restless crowd on the shore. "Surely they wouldn't dare," I muttered, more to convince myself than anything.

Kanen'tó:kon, Mohawk Observer

From my hidden vantage point near the wharf, I watched the strange scene unfold. Dozens of men, their faces smeared with soot, wearing poor imitations of my people's dress, were boarding the British ships.

I suppressed a bitter laugh. These colonists, who had taken so much from my people, now borrowed our image for their own rebellion. Yet, I couldn't help but feel a spark of satisfaction seeing them strike against their own oppressors.

The Tea

Darkness. Stillness. The gentle rocking of the ship. Then, suddenly, chaos. Crates splintered, and I felt myself lifted, carried by rough hands. For a moment, I was flying through the cold night air. Then, shockingly, I was embraced by the salty waters of the harbor. As I sank into the depths, I wondered: Was this destruction, or transformation? Was I witnessing the end of something, or the beginning?

John Hawkins

The splash of the tea crates hitting the water was oddly satisfying. All around me, my fellow Sons of Liberty worked with grim efficiency, dumping crate after crate into the harbor. No one spoke; the only sounds were the splitting of wood and the splash of tea meeting water.

As the last crate fell, a cheer went up from the shore. We had done it. We had defied the mightiest empire on earth.

William Chambers

I watched in horror as thousands of pounds of tea sank beneath the waves. Years of work, a fortune in cargo, destroyed in a matter of hours. As the "Mohawks" departed, leaving destruction in their wake, I felt a chill that had nothing to do with the December air.

"This is more than a simple riot," I murmured to Captain Hall. "This...this is the beginning of something much larger."

Kanen'tó:kon

As the false Mohawks melted back into the city, I reflected on what I had witnessed. These colonists had taken a bold step, one that would surely bring the wrath of their king upon them. I couldn't help but wonder how this would affect my people, caught between empires in a land we once called our own.

Epilogue:

In the days that followed, Boston buzzed with excitement and fear. Governor Hutchinson, furious at this blatant destruction of property, demanded immediate punishment. But the Sons of Liberty stood firm, buoyed by support from other colonies.

Across the Atlantic, news of the "tea party" would spark outrage. In the halls of Parliament, stunned silence would give way to calls for retribution. The King and his ministers would craft a response that would come to be known as the Intolerable Acts, pushing the colonies further down the path to open rebellion.

The tea that sank into Boston Harbor that night was more than just a cargo lost. It was the last dregs of colonial cooperation, giving way to a brew of revolution that would forever change the world.

Chapter 31

Liberty's Double Edge, 1774

Boston, Massachusetts - February 1774

The bitter wind whipped through the streets of Boston as I, James Freeman, a carpenter by trade and a free man of color, made my way home from a long day's work. My hands, rough from years of shaping wood, clutched a broadsheet announcing yet another protest against British taxation.

As I trudged through the snow, my mind wandered to the heated words I'd overheard at the docks earlier that day. "No taxation without representation," they'd cried. "Liberty or death!"

Liberty. The word echoed in my mind, sweet yet bitter.

I pushed open the door to my modest home, grateful for the warmth within. My wife, Sarah, looked up from her mending, her eyes questioning. "What news, James?"

I sighed, settling into a chair by the fire. "More talk of liberty and freedom from British tyranny. The Sons of Liberty are planning another demonstration."

Sarah set aside her work, her brow furrowed. "And what of our liberty, James? Will their freedom extend to our people?"

It was a question that had plagued me for months, as tensions between the colonies and Britain escalated. I had been born free in Massachusetts, had built a life and a trade for myself. Yet every day, I walked a precarious line between acceptance and suspicion, freedom and oppression.

"I don't know, my dear," I admitted. "Their words are grand, their ideals lofty. But I fear their vision of liberty may be as limited as their vision of humanity."

I thought of my friend Thomas, still enslaved on a plantation in Virginia. How could these colonists cry out against the tyranny of taxation while holding our brothers and sisters in bondage?

Yet, a part of me dared to hope. If they could challenge the might of the British Empire in the name of liberty, could that same spirit not be turned toward ending the abomination of slavery?

I rose, pacing the small room. "There's talk of a Continental Congress, of united action against British oppression. Perhaps.. .perhaps this could be an opportunity for us as well."

Sarah's eyes met mine, a mix of hope and skepticism in her gaze. "How so?"

"If they truly believe in liberty for all, then surely they must see the hypocrisy of keeping slaves. Maybe, in fighting for their own freedom, they'll come to recognize ours."

Even as I spoke the words, doubt gnawed at me. I had seen too many white faces turn away when confronted with the realities of slavery, too many grand speeches about freedom that conveniently ignored the chains binding my people.

"And if they don't?" Sarah's voice was soft but firm. "If they win their freedom and leave us in bondage?"

I had no answer for her. The truth was, I didn't know. This revolution, if it came, could be our greatest hope or our gravest threat. Would a free America extend its liberty to all, or would it enshrine the oppression of my people in a new nation's laws?

As the fire crackled in the hearth, I made a silent vow. Whatever came, I would do what I could to ensure that the voice of my people was heard. If the colonists wanted to talk about liberty, then by God, they would have to reckon with the liberty of all men, not just those with white skin.

"We must be ready," I said finally. "Ready to fight, not just for their liberty, but for our own. For Thomas, for all those still in chains, and for our children yet unborn."

Sarah nodded, reaching for my hand. In her eyes, I saw the same mixture of fear and determination that I felt in my own heart.

As the night deepened outside our little home, we sat together, contemplating the uncertain future. The drums of revolution were beating, growing louder with each passing day. And we, the free blacks of the colonies, found ourselves caught between worlds, between hope and fear, between the promise of liberty and the reality of oppression.

Whatever came, I knew one thing for certain: the fight for true freedom, for liberty for all, was far from over. Indeed, it had scarcely begun.

Chapter 32
Whispers in Versailles
Covert French Support, 1774

Versailles, France - June 15, 1774

The gilded halls of Versailles echoed with whispers of intrigue as I, François-Marie Arouet, a young diplomat newly appointed to the Foreign Ministry, hurried towards the office of the Comte de Vergennes. My heart raced with excitement and trepidation. In my hands, I clutched a report that could change the fate of nations.

As I entered the opulent chamber, I found not only the Comte but also the newly appointed Navy Minister, César Gabriel de Choiseul, deep in conversation. They fell silent at my approach.

"Ah, young Arouet," Vergennes greeted me. "What news do you bring?"

I bowed deeply. "Your Excellencies, I have here the latest dispatches from our agents in London. It seems the situation in the American colonies grows more volatile by the day."

Choiseul's eyes gleamed with interest. "Read it to us, boy."

Taking a deep breath, I began:

"The so-called 'Boston Tea Party' has inflamed tensions between Britain and her colonies. Parliament has responded with punitive measures, closing the port of Boston and restricting colonial governance. Our sources report widespread outrage among the colonists, with talk of armed resistance growing louder."

Vergennes and Choiseul exchanged meaningful glances.

"This could be the opportunity we've been waiting for," Choiseul mused. "A chance to strike at Britain's empire, to avenge our losses in the Seven Years' War."

Vergennes nodded slowly. "Perhaps. But we must tread carefully. His Majesty is young and untested. We cannot risk open warfare ...not yet."

As they debated, my mind wandered to the conversations I'd overheard in recent months. The humiliation of the Treaty of Paris in 1763 still stung. France had lost vast territories in North America and India. The desire for revenge simmered in every corner of Versailles.

"What of our American contacts?" Vergennes asked, snapping me back to attention.

"Silas Deane is expected to arrive in Paris within the month, Your Excellency," I replied. "He comes seeking covert support for the colonial cause."

Choiseul rubbed his hands together. "Excellent. We can supply them quietly, through intermediaries. Beaumarchais has already established a front company for just such a purpose."

"Roderigue Hortalez et Cie," Vergennes nodded. "Yes, that could work. We supply the colonists, weaken Britain, all without risking open war."

As the ministers continued their plotting, a wave of excitement washed over me. I was witnessing history in the making, the first moves in a grand game of international intrigue.

Months passed, and I found myself increasingly involved in the clandestine efforts to aid the American rebels. In hushed meetings and through coded messages, we arranged shipments of arms and supplies. All the while, officially, France remained neutral.

On a crisp autumn evening in 1774, I was summoned to a private audience with King Louis XVI himself. The young monarch, barely twenty years old, looked troubled as I entered his study.

"Tell me, Arouet," he said, his voice soft but commanding. "Do you believe these American rebels can truly stand against the might of Britain?"

I chose my words carefully. "Your Majesty, their cause is just, their spirit indomitable. With the right support, they may yet prevail."

Louis nodded thoughtfully. "And what of France? What is our role in this conflict?"

"Sire, we have an opportunity to reshape the balance of power in Europe and the New World. By supporting the Americans, we weaken our greatest rival. And should the colonies win their independence, we gain a valuable ally and trading partner."

The King was silent for a long moment. Finally, he spoke. "Very well. We shall continue our covert support. But remember, we must maintain plausible deniability. France cannot be seen as an aggressor."

As I left the King's presence, my mind raced with the implications of his words. France was committing itself to a dangerous game, one that could lead to glory or ruin.

In the months that followed, our efforts intensified. Ships laden with munitions and supplies sailed from French ports, ostensibly bound for the West Indies but ultimately destined for American shores. We received American agents in secret, offering encouragement and promises of support.

And all the while, we waited and watched. Would the spark of rebellion in America ignite a flame that could burn down the British Empire? Only time would tell.

As 1774 drew to a close, I stood on the balcony of Versailles, gazing out over the manicured gardens. In the distance, I could almost imagine I saw the shores of America, where a new nation was struggling to be born. And here, in the heart of the Old World, we were playing our part in that birth, for better or for worse.

The game was afoot, and France was all in, even if the world didn't know it yet. The whispers in Versailles would soon become the roar of cannons across the Atlantic. And I, François-Marie Arouet, would be there to witness it all.

Chapter 33

The Intolerable Burden, 1774

Boston, Massachusetts
August 15, 1774

My dear Cousin Thomas,

I hope this letter finds you and your family in good health. I confess it has been some time since I last wrote, but recent events have compelled me to take up my quill once more.

You have no doubt heard of the incident in our harbor last December, when a group of our more...spirited citizens decided to brew the world's largest cup of tea. While many here celebrated this act of defiance, we knew there would be consequences. Little did we imagine the severity of Parliament's response.

The so-called Coercive Acts—or as we have taken to calling them, the Intolerable Acts—have fallen upon us with the subtlety of a thunderbolt. Boston Port has been closed, Thomas, closed! Can you fathom it? Our livelihood, the very lifeblood of our town, cut off until we agree to pay for the destroyed tea. It is as if they seek to starve us into submission.

But that is not the worst of it. Our cherished Massachusetts Charter has been all but nullified. Governor Hutchinson has been recalled, replaced by General Gage, who now holds near-dictatorial powers. Our right to select our own councilors has been stripped away, and even our town meetings—the very cornerstone of our local governance—have been severely restricted.

To add insult to injury, they have begun quartering soldiers in private homes. Yes, Thomas, the very practice we protested against in '65 has returned with a vengeance. I thank Providence that our home has been spared thus far, but many of our neighbors have not been so fortunate.

Perhaps most galling of all is the Administration of Justice Act. Any official accused of a capital crime can now be transported to England for trial. They claim this is to ensure fair trials, but we all know it for what it is—a license for brutality without consequence.

I must tell you, Thomas, the mood here is grim. Many businesses have been forced to close, and unemployment grows by the day. Yet, amidst this hardship, I see something remarkable. A spirit of unity and defiance has taken hold, not just in Boston, but across the colonies.

We have received support from as far as South Carolina. Food, money, and supplies have poured in from our sister colonies. It seems Parliament's attempt to isolate us has only served to bring us closer together.

There is talk now of a Continental Congress, of colonies uniting to stand against these unjust acts. I confess, Thomas, that thoughts I would have considered treasonous mere months ago now seem not only reasonable but necessary.

I fear we are approaching a crossroads, cousin. The choices we make in the coming months may well determine the future of these colonies—whether we shall remain subjects of the British Crown or forge a new path.

I know you have always been a loyal supporter of Parliament, Thomas. I respect that, truly. But I implore you to consider our situation. Are these the actions of a just government? Can we truly be expected to surrender our rights as freeborn Englishmen without protest?

Give my love to Margaret and the children. And Thomas, please, if you have any influence in London, any way to make our voices heard, I beg you to use it. For I fear that if a peaceful resolution is not found soon, we may be headed toward a conflict from which there is no return.

Your loving cousin,

William

Chapter 34

The Tavern's Tale

First Continental Congress, 1774

Philadelphia, September 1774

If walls could talk, they say. Well, I may not have a tongue, but I've got tales to tell. I'm the City Tavern, standing proud these past twenty years on Second Street, just a stone's throw from Carpenters' Hall. I've seen my share of history, but nothing quite like this Continental Congress.

They arrived in late August and early September, these men from twelve colonies. My timbers creaked in anticipation. I'd hosted plenty of political gatherings before, but this...this was different.

First came the Virginians, led by that tall fellow, George Washington. He cut quite the figure in his officer's uniform. "No time for niceties," he said, striding past my bar. "We must prepare for war even as we hope for peace."

The Massachusetts men were next, John Adams and his cousin Samuel. Fiery ones, those two. "If Britain wants war," Samuel declared over a pint of my best ale, "then war they shall have!"

John, more measured, replied, "Peace is our first aim, cousin. But we must stand firm on our rights as Englishmen."

As September wore on, my rooms buzzed with debate. I heard talk of rights and representation, of taxes and tyranny. The Galloway Plan for colonial union was hotly debated at my tables. Joseph Galloway himself, nursing a brandy by the fire, insisted, "We must find a way to remain within the Empire!"

But John Adams, pounding my bar for emphasis, countered, "No! We must seize this moment to assert our liberties!"

I've seen divisions before—why, I remember the arguments over that blasted Stamp Act—but this was different. These men, despite their differences, were forging something new. I could feel it in my very foundations.

One night, as a storm raged outside, I overheard a group huddled in the corner. They were drafting what they called the Continental Association—an agreement to boycott British goods. My ale stocks might suffer, but I swelled with pride. These colonies, once so disparate, were coming together.

Not all was serious business, mind you. I chuckled inwardly at the cultural clashes. The New Englanders turned up their noses at the Southerners' card playing, while the Virginians found the Yankees' psalm-singing tedious. But as the weeks passed, I noticed a change. Regional drinks gave way to shared toasts. "To liberty!" they'd cry, Madeira and rum raised together.

By early October, as the Congress drew to a close, the mood had shifted. Where once I'd heard cautious talk of petitions and reconciliation, now I caught whispers of militia and munitions. Even the moderate Pennsylvanians were speaking of resistance.

On their last night, the delegates gathered in my main room. John Hancock, that wealthy Boston merchant, stood to offer a toast. "Gentlemen," he said, his voice carrying to every corner, "to a new future for these United Colonies!"

The cheer that went up shook my rafters. As they departed the next day, I knew I'd witnessed something momentous. These men had arrived as colonists from different provinces. They left as Americans, united in purpose.

In all my years, I've hosted governors and generals, merchants and ministers. But this Continental Congress...well, I reckon the echoes of their words will resound long after my last timber has crumbled to dust.

They'll be back, I'm sure of it. And when they return, this old tavern will be here, ready to host the next chapter of history. After all, revolutions may begin in council chambers, but they're fortified by good ale and spirited debate. And that, my friends, is something I know a thing or two about.

The Revolution

Chapter 35

A Sage at Sea

Benjamin Franklin's Return, 1775

Atlantic Ocean, March 21, 1775

The gentle rocking of the ship and the rhythmic splash of waves against the hull provided a soothing backdrop as I, Benjamin Franklin, put quill to paper. After nearly eleven years in London, I found myself homeward bound, my mind awash with memories and misgivings.

As England faded into the horizon behind us, I felt compelled to record my thoughts on this tumultuous period. Perhaps, in setting them down, I might make some sense of how we arrived at this precipice.

I arrived in London in 1764, full of hope and determination. The colonies were proud members of the British Empire then, and I was certain that with reason and goodwill, any misunderstandings could be resolved. How naive that now seems!

The Stamp Act crisis of 1765 should have been a warning. I remember my testimony before Parliament, trying to make them understand:

"The colonies," I told them, "are not aiming at independence. They merely seek justice and the preservation of their rights as Englishmen."

For a moment, it seemed they listened. The Act was repealed. But then came the Townshend Acts, the Boston Massacre, the Tea Act. With each new affront, I pleaded for understanding, for moderation. In drawing rooms and government offices, I argued the colonial cause. "These are your countrymen," I would say, "loyal subjects who ask only for the rights guaranteed by the British constitution."

But in the end, my words fell on deaf ears. The "Hutchinson Letters" affair was the final straw. Branded a radical and a traitor, I found myself shunned by the very society I had once moved through with ease.

Even now, as I write these words, I cling to hope. Surely, cooler heads will prevail. The bonds between Britain and her colonies are too strong, the ties of kinship and commerce too vital to be severed by these disputes. When I reach Philadelphia, I shall use whatever influence I have left to counsel patience and loyalty.

Yet a quiet voice whispers doubts in my ear. Have I underestimated the depth of colonial resentment? Has my long absence from American shores left me out of touch with the temper of my countrymen? Only time will tell.

Philadelphia, May 5, 1775

How quickly the world can change in the span of a sea voyage! I arrived in Philadelphia today, my heart light at the prospect of home and family. But the city I found was not the one I left behind all those years ago.

The streets buzz with an energy I scarcely recognize. Everywhere, talk of liberty and defiance. And then, the news that struck me like a physical blow: Lexington and Concord. Battles fought, blood spilled on American soil.

"It happened weeks ago," my son William told me, his face grave. "British troops tried to seize colonial munitions. The militia stood against them. Shots were fired. Men died."

I stood there, stunned into silence. All my years of diplomacy, all my careful arguments and reasoned pleas, swept away in a moment of gunfire and death.

"The Congress is meeting," William continued. "They're calling for volunteers, for weapons. Father, I fear this is only the beginning."

As the full impact of the news washed over me, I felt a profound shift in my understanding. The America I left behind, the loyal colonial subjects I had championed in London, were gone. In their place stood a people awakening to a new identity, forged in resistance and, now, in blood.

I thought back to my hopeful musings aboard the ship, and a rueful smile crossed my lips. How quickly my words had become relics of a bygone era! The time for moderation, for appeals to British sensibilities, had passed. A new chapter in history had begun, and I found myself thrust into its pages, ready or not.

That night, as I prepared for bed in a city thrumming with nervous energy, I pondered my place in this brave new world. I had sailed from London as a loyal, if disgruntled, British subject. I arrived in Philadelphia as...what? A revolutionary? A traitor? A patriot?

One thing was clear: the America I had returned to was not the one I had left. And I, Benjamin Franklin, would have to chart a new course in these uncharted waters.

As I drifted off to sleep, the distant echo of militia drums mingled with my thoughts. The shot fired at Lexington had indeed been heard 'round the world. And its echoes, I feared, would shake the very foundations of the British Empire.

Chapter 36

The Night of Whispers
Paul Revere and Company, 1775

Boston and surrounding areas, April 18-19, 1775

Dr. Joseph Warren - Boston, 9:00 PM, April 18

The candle flickered as I, Dr. Joseph Warren, penned the last of my instructions. The intelligence was clear: the British were on the move. Their target: our weapon stores in Concord.

I looked up at the two men before me - Paul Revere and William Dawes. Trust and determination shone in their eyes.

"Gentlemen," I said, my voice low, "you know your routes. Revere, by sea to Charlestown, then on to Lexington. Dawes, by land through Roxbury. Warn Adams and Hancock, then press on to Concord. Tell them: 'The Regulars are coming out.'"

They nodded, understanding the gravity of their mission. As they turned to leave, I added, "Godspeed, and remember—we are not alone in this endeavor."

Robert Newman - Old North Church, 10:00 PM, April 18

My heart pounded as I climbed the stairs of the Old North Church, two lanterns clutched in my sweating hands. As sexton, I had the keys, but never had they felt so heavy.

Reaching the belfry, I peered out into the night. Boston was eerily quiet, unaware of the storm about to break. With trembling hands, I hung the lanterns. "One if by land, two if by sea," Revere had said.

I stepped back, watching the flames dance. Two lanterns, signaling the British were rowing across the Charles River. In those small lights, I saw the spark of revolution.

William Dawes - Roxbury, 11:30 PM, April 18

The sound of my horse's hooves seemed impossibly loud in the night. Every shadow could be a British patrol, every rustle a potential ambush. But I, William Dawes, pressed on.

Through Roxbury and into Cambridge, I rode. At each home of a trusted patriot, I rapped on the door, whispering urgently, "The Regulars are coming out. Muster your militia."

Sleepy faces turned alert, candles were lit, and soon, I could hear the drum of alarm behind me as I rode on.

Paul Revere - Charlestown to Lexington, Midnight, April 19

The boat's oars cut silently through the dark waters of the Charles. On the opposite shore, I could see the lanterns shining in the Old North Church. Two lights—the British were coming by sea.

Landing in Charlestown, I quickly secured a horse. "The Regulars are coming out," I told the stable master. He nodded grimly, already reaching for his musket.

I rode hard for Lexington, stopping at farmhouses along the way. "Alarm the countryside," I urged. "The Regulars are out."

Various Colonists - Towns between Boston and Concord, 12:30 AM - 1:30 AM, April 19

In Menotomy (now Arlington), Reverend Clark stirred at the urgent knocking. "The alarm's been given," a breathless messenger said. "Regulars marching on Concord."

In Lexington, John Hancock paced nervously as Samuel Adams urged calm. "We must trust in Providence and our fellow patriots," Adams said.

On a small farm outside of Lincoln, young Ruth Baker watched her father grab his musket. "Bar the door after me," he told her mother. "The Regulars are out, and every man is needed."

Dr. Samuel Prescott - Lincoln to Concord, 1:45 AM, April 19

I hadn't expected to be part of history that night. I, Dr. Samuel Prescott, was simply returning home from courting my love in Lexington when I encountered Revere and Dawes on the road.

"The Regulars are out," they told me. Instinctively, I knew I had to help.

When we were ambushed by a British patrol, I managed to escape. Revere and Dawes were captured, but the message must get through. I spurred my horse towards Concord, determined to finish what they had started.

Pounding on doors, I spread the alarm. "To arms!" I cried. "The Regulars are coming out!"

As dawn broke over Concord, I saw hundreds of militia assembling on the green. The alarm had been sounded, the countryside roused. Whatever happened next, we would face it together.

Epilogue:

By sunrise on April 19, 1775, the entire countryside from Boston to Concord was awake and armed. The midnight ride—not of one man, but of many—had succeeded. As the British column marched out of Boston, they found not sleeping villages, but a colony ready to fight for its liberty.

The first shots of the American Revolution were about to be fired, and it was the courage and dedication of many ordinary colonists that had made it possible. The night of whispers had become the dawn of revolution.

Chapter 37

The Shot Heard Round the World

The Battle of Lexington and Concord, April 1775

Lexington, Massachusetts - April 19, 1775

Darkness. Stillness. These were my constants. Then, suddenly, movement. I was plucked from my fellows, held for a moment in warm flesh before being dropped into a cold metal tube. Was this my purpose? My destiny?

A deafening roar, and I was flying. The world blurred around me, a chaos of colors and shapes. Men in red coats. Others in plain clothes. Faces contorted with fear, anger, determination. I had no time to ponder as I hurtled through the morning air.

Impact. Pain. Not mine, for I feel nothing, but the man I struck cried out as he fell. Red blossomed on his chest where I entered. Was this what I was made for? To tear flesh and spill blood?

As the man's life ebbed away, I found myself pondering. Who had fired me? The soldier in red or the farmer in homespun? Did it matter? I had done what bullets do, yet I felt...uncertain.

Around me, chaos erupted. More of my kind flew through the air, each finding its mark in wood, earth, or flesh. Men shouted, horses whinnied in fear, the acrid smell of gunpowder filled the air. This, then, was battle.

But was I just another bullet, or was I something more? They would call me "the shot heard round the world," but in that moment, I was simply a lump of lead, doing what lead does when propelled by powder and sparks.

Should I feel pride? I had struck the first blow in what would become a great conflict, a struggle for liberty that would echo through the ages. Nations would be born from the chaos I unleashed.

Or should I feel sorrow? For I was the first of countless bullets that would fly before this war was done. How many lives would be cut short, how many families torn apart, all starting with my flight?

Perhaps it was neither pride nor sorrow I should feel, but a sort of resigned acceptance. I did not choose to be fired, did not choose my target. I was an instrument of fate, a physical manifestation of tensions long simmering between colony and crown.

Was it luck that made me the first, or was it destiny? Would history have changed if I had flown a few inches to the left or right? Or was this moment inevitable, my flight merely the spark that lit a powder keg primed to explode?

As the battle raged around my resting place, I contemplated the future I had set in motion. I saw armies clashing on battlefields yet to be named, great men rising to lead a nation not yet born. I saw a world forever changed by the revolution I had begun.

But I also saw the cost. The blood that would soak the earth, the lives cut short, the families shattered. Was freedom worth such a price? It was not for me, a mere bullet, to decide.

In the end, I was both more and less than "the shot heard round the world." I was a simple lump of lead that did what lead does. Yet

I was also the beginning of something momentous, the first note in a symphony of liberty that would play out across continents and centuries.

As the sun rose higher over Lexington, as men fought and died around me, I rested in the flesh I had pierced, a silent witness to the birth of a nation. The shot had been fired, the world had heard, and nothing would ever be the same again.

Chapter 38

A Tavern's Tale: The Birth of a Nation

Second Continental Congress, May – July 1775

Philadelphia, May - July 1775

I am the City Tavern, and once again, my walls echo with the whispers of revolution. The Second Continental Congress has convened, and the tension in the air is palpable.

They arrive in twos and threes, these delegates from thirteen colonies. Some faces I recognize from the First Continental Congress—the firebrand John Adams, the eloquent Thomas Jefferson. Others are new, their expressions a mix of determination and apprehension.

As they gather around my tables, nursing ales and whiskeys, I hear snippets of their conversations. The war that began at Lexington and Concord weighs heavily on their minds.

"We need a united front," I hear John Hancock declare. "This Congress must act as one body for all the colonies."

And act they do. Day after day, they meet at the Pennsylvania State House, but it's within my walls that the real debates take place. I watch as they transform from a group of colonial representatives into something more—the seeds of a new government.

They establish the Continental Army, a bold move that speaks of their commitment to this conflict. They debate issues of trade and diplomacy, grappling with the realities of governing a nation at war.

"We're no longer just seeking reconciliation," Benjamin Franklin muses one evening. "We're laying the groundwork for independence, whether we admit it or not."

I've seen my share of political gatherings, but this is different. These men aren't just discussing grievances or drafting petitions. They're creating something entirely new—a government that spans from New Hampshire to Georgia, united in its defiance of British rule.

They issue paper money, establish a postal service, and send diplomats to seek foreign support. With each decision, they move further from their identity as British subjects and closer to something else - Americans.

As the summer wears on, I notice a change in the delegates. The weight of their responsibilities shows in the lines on their faces, the intensity of their discussions. They understand that their actions here, in this tavern and in the State House down the street, are shaping the future of a continent.

One night, as the delegates prepare to adjourn for the evening, I overhear a conversation between John Adams and his cousin Samuel.

"We're no longer just a Congress," John says quietly. "We've become a government in all but name."

Samuel nods, his eyes gleaming. "A government of a new nation, John. One that's yet to be born, but whose first cries we can already hear."

As they leave, I stand silent in the warm Philadelphia night. I've been a witness to history before, but this...this is something different. Within my walls, and in the chambers of the State House, a new nation is taking its first breaths.

The Second Continental Congress may not have declared independence yet, but in their actions, in their assumption of the powers of governance, they've taken the first steps on the road to nationhood. And I, the humble City Tavern, have had the privilege of hosting this remarkable transformation.

The journey is far from over, I know. There will be more debates, more decisions, perhaps even open war. But whatever comes, I'll be here, ready to offer a warm hearth and a cool drink to those who would forge a new nation.

Chapter 39

The Hill of Reckoning

The Battle of Bunker Hill, 1775

Boston, June 17, 1775

General William Howe:

From my vantage point in Boston, I survey the growing menace across the harbor. The rebels have been busy, their earthworks sprouting like weeds around the city. This siege cannot stand. We must act decisively.

My gaze settles on the promontories of the Charlestown peninsula—Bunker Hill and Breed's Hill. If the rebels seize that high ground, our position in Boston will become untenable. We cannot allow it.

I turn to my staff. "Gentlemen, we attack at first light. We'll land at Moulton's Point and drive these colonial upstarts from the heights. By tomorrow evening, the hills will be ours."

As my officers disperse to prepare, I can't help but feel a twinge of anticipation. Finally, a chance to show these rebels the might of the British Army.

Colonel William Prescott:

The night is alive with the sound of shovels and pickaxes as we fortify our position on Breed's Hill. Some of the men grumble, wondering why we're not on Bunker Hill as originally ordered. I've explained our reasoning—Breed's Hill is closer to Boston, a more threatening position—but doubts linger.

"Keep at it, men," I encourage, moving among the workers. "We must have these defenses ready by dawn."

I can see the British warships in the harbor, ominous in the moonlight. They'll be coming for us, no doubt about that. But we'll be ready. We must be.

General Howe:

The morning sun glints off the waters of the harbor as our boats make for the Charlestown shore. From my position in the lead craft, I can see the rebel fortifications clearly now. Impressive work for one night, I must admit.

As we land at Moulton's Point, I order the troops to form up. The rebels watch us from their entrenchments, maddeningly passive. No matter. We'll soon flush them out.

"Forward, men of the King! Show these traitors the steel of British bayonets!"

Colonel Prescott:

The British are coming. I can see their red coats, bright against the green grass as they form their lines. My men shift nervously, fingers tightening on their muskets.

"Steady, lads," I call out. "Wait for my order. *Don't fire until you see the whites of their eyes!*"

It's a necessity born of our limited ammunition as much as tactics, but the men nod grimly, understanding.

The British advance up the hill, their lines impressively straight. Closer...closer...

"Fire!"

The world erupts in smoke and thunder.

General Howe:

I watch in horror as the first ranks of our attack crumble under the rebels' volley. Men I've known for years fall, clutching at ghastly wounds. For a moment, I'm back on the Plains of Abraham, watching Wolfe fall. But there's no time for such thoughts.

"Reform the lines!" I bellow. "We'll try again!"

But as we launch our second assault, a terrible thought gnaws at me. What if we've underestimated these colonials?

Colonel Prescott:

We've repulsed two assaults now, but our situation grows desperate. Ammunition runs low, and the men are exhausted. The British will come again, I'm sure of it.

"Check every cartridge box," I order. "Gather ammunition from the fallen. We must hold this position!"

Even as I speak, I see the British lines reforming. How long can we hold out?

General Howe:

The hills are littered with our dead and wounded, the air thick with smoke and the cries of the injured. But we cannot fail. One more push, that's all we need.

"Once more, men!" I call out, my voice hoarse. "For King and Country!"

As we advance up the slope once more, I pray this will be the last time.

Colonel Prescott:

Our powder is almost gone. The British swarm up the hill, and this time, we have no answer for them.

"Fall back!" I order, my heart heavy. "Make for Bunker Hill!"

As we retreat, I look back at our position, now swarming with redcoats. We've lost the hill, but by God, we've bled them for it.

General Howe:

At last, the heights are ours. But as I stand amid the carnage, surrounded by the moans of the wounded and dying, victory tastes like ashes.

Over a thousand casualties. A third of my force. All to take a hill that the rebels had occupied for less than a day.

If this is what it will take to subdue the colonies, I fear this war will be long and bloody indeed.

Colonel Prescott:

As night falls, I gather with the other officers to take stock. We've lost the hill, but the cost to the British was enormous. More importantly, we've shown that we can stand toe-to-toe with the finest army in the world.

This battle may have been lost, but a new spirit has been born this day. The cause of liberty has been baptized in fire and blood on the slopes of Breed's Hill. And I fear this is only the beginning.

Chapter 40

The Weight of Command

George Washington – Commander-in-Chief, 1775

Philadelphia, June 19, 1775 - Evening

The door of the City Tavern swung open, admitting a tall, imposing figure. George Washington ducked slightly to clear the doorframe, his eyes adjusting to the smoky interior. No sooner had he stepped inside than a chorus of voices rang out.

"There he is!"

"To our new Commander-in-Chief!"

"Come join us, George!"

Washington managed a small smile, nodding to his enthusiastic colleagues from the Continental Congress. John Adams raised a glass in his direction, beaming with pride at the nomination he had so ardently supported.

"Gentlemen," Washington said, his voice carrying over the din, "I thank you for your kind wishes. I would be glad to join you shortly, but if you'll excuse me, I find I need a moment to collect my thoughts."

Understanding nods and murmurs of assent followed. Washington made his way to the bar, ordered a glass of Madeira, and found a quiet corner table. As he sat, the weight of the day's events seemed to settle upon his shoulders like a physical burden.

Commander-in-Chief of the Continental Army. The words echoed in his mind as he sipped his wine.

Am I truly ready for this? he wondered. His military experience in the French and Indian War seemed paltry compared to the task that now lay before him. To lead an army against the might of the British Empire—it was a daunting prospect, to say the least.

Washington's mind raced with the challenges ahead. He would need to mold a cohesive fighting force out of disparate colonial militias. Men from Massachusetts would need to serve alongside those from Georgia, New Hampshire volunteers with Virginians. Could he forge them into a united army?

And what of supplies? Already he had heard reports of shortages—gunpowder, muskets, even shoes. How does one wage war without the tools of war?

Then there was the matter of experience. The British Army was the finest in the world, led by seasoned commanders. In comparison, his own military knowledge felt woefully inadequate. "I fear this may be too much for my abilities," he murmured softly, echoing the words he had spoken to Patrick Henry earlier that day.

Yet, as Washington gazed into his glass, he felt a steely resolve begin to form. The Congress had chosen him, unanimously. They believed in him, and he could not - would not - let them down. More importantly, he could not let down the cause of liberty, for which so much had already been sacrificed.

His thoughts turned to Mount Vernon, to Martha. Accepting this command meant leaving behind the life he loved, potentially for years. But then, sacrifice was the order of the day, was it not? How could he ask soldiers to leave their homes and families if he was unwilling to do the same?

The fate of a nation yet unborn rested on his shoulders. The thought was at once terrifying and exhilarating. Win or lose, the outcome of this conflict would reshape the world. And he, George Washington, would play a central role in determining that outcome.

"So be it," Washington said softly, draining the last of his Madeira. He stood, squaring his shoulders. Whatever doubts he might harbor, whatever challenges lay ahead, he would meet them head-on. The Congress, the Army, the people—they needed a leader who exuded confidence and resolve. He would be that leader.

As he made his way back to his colleagues, their cheerful voices rising to greet him, Washington allowed himself a small smile. The path ahead was uncertain, fraught with danger and hardship. But it was a path he would walk willingly, for the sake of liberty and the future of America.

"Gentlemen," he said as he reached the table, his voice strong and clear, "I thank you for the trust you have placed in me. Now, let us discuss the work that lies ahead. We have an army to build and a war to win."

As cheers erupted around him, Washington felt the weight of command settle firmly upon him. It was a burden he would bear with honor, dignity, and unwavering resolve. The fight for American independence had truly begun.

Chapter 41

A King's Resolve

The Royal Proclamation of Rebellion, 1775

St. James's Palace, London, August 23, 1775

I, George the Third, by the Grace of God, King of Great Britain, France, and Ireland, Defender of the Faith, stand before the ornate mirror in my private chambers, adjusting the powdered wig that sits heavily upon my brow. Today, I shall make known my will to all the world, to put an end to this colonial mischief once and for all.

My secretary, William, waits patiently, quill poised over parchment. I clear my throat and begin to dictate:

"Whereas many of our subjects in divers parts of our Colonies and Plantations in North America, misled by dangerous and ill-designing men, and forgetting the allegiance which they owe to the power that has protected and supported them, after various disorderly acts committed in disturbance of the public peace, to the obstruction of lawful commerce, and to the oppression of our loyal subjects carrying on the same, have at length proceeded to an open and avowed rebellion..."

Rebellion. The word tastes bitter on my tongue. How has it come to this? These colonists, ungrateful children of the Empire, daring to raise arms against their mother country. Do they not understand the natural order of things?

I continue: "...by arraying themselves in hostile manner to withstand the execution of the law, and traitorously preparing, ordering, and levying war against us."

I pause in my dictation, pacing the length of my chamber, my mind racing. Reports of Lexington and Concord still ring in my ears. British blood spilled on colonial soil. It is intolerable.

Returning to my proclamation, I resume: "And whereas there is reason to apprehend that such rebellion hath been much promoted and encouraged by the traitorous correspondence, counsels, and comfort of divers wicked and desperate persons within this realm..."

My thoughts turn to those troublemakers in Parliament. Pitt, Burke, and their ilk. Always arguing for leniency, for understanding. Bah! What is needed now is strength, resolve.

"To the end therefore that none of our subjects may neglect or violate their duty through ignorance thereof, or through any doubt of the protection which the law will afford to their loyalty and zeal; we have thought fit, by and with the advice of our Privy Council, to issue this our Royal Proclamation, hereby declaring that not only all our officers civil and military are obliged to exert their utmost endeavours to suppress such rebellion, and to bring the traitors to justice..."

Yes, justice. These rebels must be made to understand the consequences of their actions. The might of the British Empire will be brought to bear, and order will be restored.

I conclude: "...but that all our subjects of this realm and the dominions thereunto belonging are bound by law to be aiding and assisting in the suppression of such rebellion, and to disclose and make known all traitorous conspiracies and attempts against us, our crown and dignity..."

As William scribes the final words, I feel the weight of history upon my shoulders. I am George III, King of the mightiest empire the world has ever known. I shall not be the monarch who loses the American colonies. Whatever the cost, whatever it takes, I shall see this rebellion crushed and proper order restored.

For King and Country, for the very future of the Empire, it must be so.

Chapter 42

Freedom's Call

Lord Dunmore's Proclamation, Nov. 1775

Norfolk, Virginia - November 1775

The first whispers reached us in the fields, carried on the autumn wind like seeds of hope. At first, I, Elijah, dared not believe it. After twenty-three years of bondage, hope was a dangerous thing.

"Lord Dunmore's offered freedom," Old Sam murmured as we worked the tobacco rows. "To any slave willin' to fight for the British."

I paused, my hoe suspended mid-air. "What you mean, Old Sam?"

He glanced around, making sure no overseer was within earshot. "The Governor, he's put out a proclamation. Says any able-bodied Negro joinin' His Majesty's troops will be free."

That night, as we huddled in our quarters, the talk was of nothing else. Freedom. The word hung in the air, tantalizing and terrifying all at once.

"It's a trick," warned Bessie, her eyes narrowed with suspicion. "White folks don't give nothin' for free."

But Joshua, young and full of fire, argued back. "And what if it ain't? What if this is our chance?"

I said nothing, my mind racing. I thought of my wife, Sarah, and our little girl, both sold away two summers past. Of the scars on my back from the overseer's whip. Of the crushing weight of knowing that my life, my very being, belonged to another.

Days passed, and more news trickled in. We heard that slaves were fleeing plantations all across Virginia, making their way to Norfolk where Lord Dunmore was raising his "Ethiopian Regiment."

Master Harrison was in a rage. "Dunmore's a traitor," he spat over dinner, loud enough for us serving to hear. "Inciting servile insurrection. He'll hang for this!"

But the fire had been lit. That very night, Joshua disappeared. Then two more the next week. Each escape stoked the flames of possibility in my heart.

It was Ruth, the house slave, who finally brought us a copy of the proclamation itself. She'd snatched it from the master's study, risking a severe beating if caught.

By the light of a smuggled candle, those of us who could read pored over the words:

"I do hereby further declare all indentured servants, Negroes, or others, (appertaining to Rebels,) free that are able and willing to bear Arms, they joining His Majesty's Troops."

The words sang of freedom, yet the limitations were clear. Only those belonging to "rebels"—those fighting against the British. Only those able to bear arms.

"What about the women? The children? The old folks?" I wondered aloud.

Old Sam shook his head. "It ain't about us, son. It's about them winning their war."

And yet, for all its limitations, the proclamation had done something remarkable. It had given us choice. For the first time in my life, I had a decision to make. Stay in the familiar bonds of slavery, or risk everything for a chance at freedom.

As dawn broke, I made my choice. With nothing but the clothes on my back and a desperate hope in my heart, I slipped away from the plantation.

The road to Norfolk was long and fraught with danger. Slave patrols were out in force, and every white face was a potential threat. But the thought of freedom, of holding my head high as a man and not property, drove me onward.

When I finally reached the British lines, I was exhausted, hungry, and terrified. A soldier eyed me suspiciously.

"You here for Lord Dunmore's regiment?" he asked.

I stood as straight as I could, finding a courage I didn't know I possessed. "Yes, sir. I'm here to fight. For my freedom."

As they led me to the Ethiopian Regiment, I saw faces black as mine wearing British uniforms, standing tall and proud. For the first time, I allowed myself to truly believe. Freedom was more than a whisper now. It was a possibility. A future I could grasp with my own two hands.

I didn't know what battles lay ahead, or whether we would win or lose. I didn't know if the British would keep their promise if victory was theirs. But I knew that for the first time in my life, I was taking a step of my own choosing.

As I donned the uniform of the Ethiopian Regiment, I silently vowed that whatever came, I would never be a slave again. Lord Dunmore's Proclamation had opened a door, and I had walked through it into a new, uncertain, but free world.

Chapter 43

The Power of Words

Common Sense,
Philadelphia – January 1776

Thomas Paine hunched over his desk, surrounded by crumpled papers, candlelight flickering across his fevered scribbling. The hour was late, but the words flowed like a river unleashed.

"In the following pages, I offer nothing more than simple facts, plain arguments, and common sense..."

He paused, considering. Yes, that was right. No flowery language, no Latin phrases to impress the educated. This was for the common man, the farmer, the tradesman, the shopkeeper.

"The sun never shined on a cause of greater worth..."

Paine dipped his quill again, his mind racing. How to explain complex political theory to people who'd never read Locke or Rousseau? Ah, yes—use what they know.

"Society in every state is a blessing, but government even in its best state is but a necessary evil; in its worst state an intolerable one..."

Perfect. Simple, clear, undeniable. Now, to tackle monarchy. Again, use the familiar...

"For all men being originally equals, no one by birth could have a right to set up his own family in perpetual preference to all others forever..."

He smiled grimly. Let King George chew on that.

The Bull's Head Tavern, Boston - Two Weeks Later

James Murphy wiped down his bar, watching the growing crowd with interest. Ever since he'd gotten his hands on that pamphlet, "Common Sense," his tavern had been packed. Every night, someone would read passages aloud, and the debates would begin.

Tonight was no different. Samuel Cooper, a local schoolteacher, stood on a chair, holding the well-worn pamphlet.

"Listen to this," he called out. "'.'*A long habit of not thinking a thing wrong, gives it a superficial appearance of being right..*"

"Aye," called out John Webb, a weathered farmer. "Like paying taxes to a king three thousand miles away who's never set foot on our soil!"

Murphy noticed William Ashworth, a known loyalist, shift uncomfortably in his corner.

"And this part," Cooper continued, "'*The period of debate is closed. Arms, as the last resource, decide the contest...*'"

"He's right," declared Mary Thompson, Murphy's cook. "My boys need to know if they're British subjects or free men. Can't keep straddling that fence forever."

"But what of the consequences?" Ashworth finally spoke up. "To break with England—it's madness!"

Cooper turned the page. *"The blood of the slain, the weeping voice of nature cries, 'TIS TIME TO PART.'"*

A murmur ran through the crowd. Murphy watched faces change as the words sank in—doubt turning to conviction, fear to resolve.

Paine's Lodgings

"Three shillings a copy," Paine muttered, reviewing the printer's bill. "Keep it cheap, let it spread."

He'd heard his words were being read in taverns across the colonies. The thought both thrilled and terrified him. This wasn't just political theory anymore—these words could change the course of history.

"O ye that love mankind!" he had written. *"Ye that dare oppose not only the tyranny, but the tyrant, stand forth!"*

Stand forth indeed. His pen had lit a fire. Now to see what burned in its wake.

The Bull's Head Tavern - Late Evening

Murphy watched his last customers leave, still arguing about the pamphlet's ideas. Even Ashworth had grown quiet, thoughtful.

"It's not the words themselves," Murphy's wife Sarah observed, helping him clean up. "It's how he says them. Makes it all so clear, so obvious. Makes you wonder why we never saw it this way before."

Murphy nodded, picking up the much-handled copy of "Common Sense" from a table. Independence. Just weeks ago, it had seemed unthinkable. Now? Now it seemed inevitable.

"The cause of America is in a great measure the cause of all mankind..." he read softly.

Outside his tavern, a new world was being born, midwifed by the power of words that any person could understand. Common sense, indeed.

Paine's Lodgings

In his lodgings, Thomas Paine finally set down his quill. The words were out there now, spreading like wildfire through the colonies. Simple words, plain arguments, common sense—weapons more powerful than any musket or cannon.

He had done what he could. Now it was up to the people to decide. Would they stand forth? Would they dare to imagine a world without kings?

Only time would tell. But as he looked out his window at the pre-dawn sky, Thomas Paine allowed himself to hope. The sun never shined on a cause of greater worth, indeed.

Chapter 44

In Congress, July 4, 1776

Part I: The Writer

Late June, 1776 - Philadelphia

I, Thomas Jefferson, sit at my desk in my rented rooms, the weight of history bearing down upon my quill. The committee has entrusted me with drafting this Declaration, though I suspect Adams pushed for my selection mainly to avoid the task himself.

The words flow more easily than I expected:

"When in the Course of human events, it becomes necessary for one people to dissolve the political bands which have connected them with another..."

I pause, considering the enormity of what we propose. Not just independence, but a complete reimagining of governance itself.

"We hold these truths to be self-evident, that all men are created equal..."

My hand trembles slightly as I write these words. The hypocrisy of my position is not lost on me. How can I, a man who owns other human beings, declare that all men are created equal? Yet the truth of these words burns in my soul, even as I fail to live up to them.

I continue writing, my quill scratching against parchment:

"He has waged cruel war against human nature itself, violating its most sacred rights of life and liberty in the persons of a distant people who never offended him, carrying them into slavery in another hemisphere..."

This passage, denouncing the slave trade, will never survive the committee's review, particularly from our southern delegates. Yet I must include it. The contradiction between our words and our actions must be acknowledged, even if only in this first draft.

Part II: The Vote

July 2, 1776 - Independence Hall

John Adams:

The debate has been fierce, but at last, the moment has arrived. I can barely contain my excitement as the roll call begins.
New Hampshire? "Aye."
Massachusetts? "Aye."
Rhode Island? "Aye."
Down the list we go, each colony adding its voice. Even New York, which had abstained until now, joins the chorus.
It is done. We have voted for independence.
Later that evening, I write to my beloved Abigail: "The Second Day of July 1776 will be the most memorable epoch in the History

of America... It ought to be solemnized with Pomp and Parade, with Shows, Games, Sports, Guns, Bells, Bonfires and Illuminations from one End of this Continent to the other from this Time forward forever more."

Little do I know that it will be July 4th, not July 2nd, that history remembers.

Part III: The Editing

July 3-4, 1776 - Independence Hall

Thomas Jefferson:

I sit, seething quietly as they dissect my work. Word by word, line by line, they debate and alter my carefully crafted text.

My passage on slavery - gone. My most impassioned denouncements of the British people - moderated. My poetic flourishes - simplified.

Benjamin Franklin leans over, noticing my distress. "When you write for others, Thomas," he whispers, "you must let them make it their own."

I know he's right, but each change feels like a knife in my gut. Yet as I listen to the debate, I begin to understand. This document must represent not one man's views, but a nation's. Its words must survive not just today's passions, but stand the test of time.

Part IV: The Signing

August 2, 1776 - Independence Hall

Benjamin Franklin:

The large parchment lies before us, Hancock's bold signature already commanding attention at the top. One by one, we step forward to add our names.

"We must all hang together," I quip to the assembled delegates, "or assuredly we shall all hang separately."

A few nervous chuckles greet my gallows humor, but the gravity of the moment is not lost on anyone. This is not just a declaration—it is our death warrant if we fail.

I watch young Thomas Lynch struggle to steady his hand as he signs. Harrison jokes about his weight as he affixes his name. Each man approaches the task differently, but all understand—there is no turning back now.

Epilogue: The Document

From the Archives of Time

I am but parchment and ink, yet I carry within me the hopes and dreams of a nation. My words, debated, edited, and ultimately approved, would echo through centuries:

"We hold these truths to be self-evident, that all men are created equal, that they are endowed by their Creator with certain unalienable Rights, that among these are Life, Liberty and the pursuit of Happiness."

My promises remain unfulfilled, my ideals not yet fully realized. The man who wrote me owned slaves. The men who signed me represented only a fraction of the population. Yet my words have inspired struggles for freedom far beyond what my creators imagined.

I am both a birth certificate and a promissory note—declaring not just independence from Britain, but independence from tyranny in all its forms. My work is not yet done, my promises not yet kept. But as long as people yearn for freedom, my words will continue to echo:

"...And for the support of this Declaration, with a firm reliance on the protection of divine Providence, we mutually pledge to each other our Lives, our Fortunes and our sacred Honor."

Chapter 45

Echoes of Independence

Savannah, Georgia – August 1776

The town hall was packed to the rafters as I, James Johnston, printer of the Georgia Gazette, watched the crowd gather. The Declaration had come off my press just hours ago, the ink barely dry. Now, copies circulated through the assembly as Button Gwinnett, our own delegate to Congress, prepared to read it aloud.

Strange to think that these words, which I had painstakingly set in type, could change the very fabric of our society. Stranger still to realize that here, in the youngest and most loyal of colonies, we were about to publicly cast off our ties to the Crown.

"When in the Course of human events..." Gwinnett began.

I studied the faces around me. Old Thomas Bradford, the merchant, crumpled his copy in disgust and stormed out. No surprise there—half his family still lived in England, and his business depended on British trade.

But Sarah Miller, whose husband's shop had suffered under the various acts and taxes, listened with shining eyes. Their son had already joined the militia.

"We hold these truths to be self-evident, that all men are created equal..."

"Equal?" muttered James McIntosh, a prominent planter. "What dangerous nonsense is this?" Several of his fellow planters nodded in agreement. They had the most to lose if such ideas spread too far.

Yet beside them stood William McCall, another planter, nodding thoughtfully. "It's not about that kind of equality," he whispered to his nervous colleagues. "It's about our equal rights as Englishmen—rights the King has violated."

"A Prince, whose character is thus marked by every act which may define a Tyrant, is unfit to be the ruler of a free people."

Martha Burney, the tavern keeper's wife, gasped. "That's treason!" she exclaimed.

"It certainly is," replied old Reverend Coates. "The question, my dear, is whether it's justified treason."

I watched young Timothy Greene, barely seventeen, hanging on every word. His father had been killed by Creek Indians two years ago. "But who'll protect us from the Spanish in Florida?" he asked. "Or the Indians on the frontier?"

"We'll protect ourselves," declared James Jackson, a fiery youth who'd been drilling with the militia. "Better to face those threats as free men than live as slaves to Britain."

As Gwinnett read on, I noticed how the mood in the room began to shift. The initial shock of the Declaration's bold pronouncements gave way to thoughtful consideration. Even some who had initially recoiled seemed to be weighing the arguments more carefully.

"And for the support of this Declaration, with a firm reliance on the protection of Divine Providence, we mutually pledge to each other our Lives, our Fortunes, and our sacred Honor."

A long silence followed the final words. Then Joseph Clay, a prominent merchant, stood up.

"I've long opposed breaking with Britain," he said slowly. "The risks seemed too great. But we can't go back now. The question is no longer whether independence is wise, but whether we stand together or fall separately."

"Easy for you to say," called out William Belcher, a small farmer. "You've got money set aside. Some of us will starve if the British blockade our ports."

"We might starve if we stay with Britain too," countered Mary Rogers, the baker's wife. "Their blockade is already squeezing us, and we're still their 'loyal subjects.'"

As the debate continued, I noticed groups forming—not just along the usual social lines, but mixing in new ways. Planters deep in discussion with craftsmen. Merchants arguing points with farmers. Women joining in the debates as readily as men.

Something was happening here, something more than just a political discussion. These people, my neighbors, were no longer just inhabitants of a British colony. They were becoming citizens of a new nation, wrestling with what that meant.

Late into the night, the debates continued. Not everyone was convinced—some would never be. But as I walked home in the warm Georgia night, my printing press silent for the first time in days, I reflected on what I had witnessed.

We were no longer just Georgia, the youngest and most loyal colony. We were becoming something new - Americans. The Declaration I had printed was more than just words on paper. It was a birth certificate for a nation, and tonight I had watched that nation take its first breaths.

Tomorrow, I would print the news of this meeting. Let the record show that even here, in distant Georgia, independence had found its voice. Let it show that we too had pledged our lives, our fortunes, and our sacred honor to this bold new experiment in liberty.

The die was cast. For better or worse, we were all rebels now.

Chapter 46

The Escape from Brooklyn

Long Island, August 27, 1776

General William Howe watched with satisfaction as his troops executed the night march perfectly. Through the Jamaica Pass they went, quiet as ghosts, guided by local Loyalists who knew every trail. Dawn would find them behind the rebel lines, a textbook flanking maneuver.

"Perfect," he murmured. "Simply perfect."

Memories of Bunker Hill tempered his satisfaction. The rebels had proven they could fight, and he had the scars to prove it. No, there would be no headlong assault this time. Methodical. Professional. That was the way to crush this rebellion.

George Washington peered through his spyglass at the British lines before Brooklyn Heights. Something wasn't right. The enemy seemed too quiet, their front lines too thin.

A rider galloped up. "Sir! The British! They're behind us!"

Washington's blood ran cold. Howe had done it—outflanked them completely. Even now, he could see his left wing collapsing, men running in panic as the British appeared where no British should be.

"Order Sullivan and Stirling to hold as long as they can," he commanded. "We must protect the retreat to Brooklyn Heights."

But as the day wore on, the situation grew desperate. Washington watched helplessly as more of his army was chewed up, surrounded, captured. His first major battle as Commander-in-Chief was becoming a disaster.

Howe surveyed the rebel fortifications on Brooklyn Heights. One good assault might carry them, but at what cost? No, better to do this properly. Bring up the artillery, lay siege. The rebels were trapped between his army and the East River. They weren't going anywhere.

"General," his aide suggested, "shouldn't we press the attack?"

Howe shook his head. "Let's not have another Bunker Hill. We'll do this methodically."

Washington paced the American lines as darkness fell. The British were digging siege works. Soon, their ships would sail up the East River, cutting off any escape.

Unless...

He called for Colonel John Glover, commander of the Marblehead Regiment. The weathered fisherman arrived quickly.

"Colonel, we need boats. Every boat you can find. And men who know how to use them."

Glover's eyes gleamed with understanding. "My Marblehead men were born on the water, sir. We'll get it done."

Through the night, Washington watched as Glover's men worked miracles. Fishing boats, merchant skiffs, anything that could float was pressed into service. In absolute silence, they began ferrying the army across the East River.

Regiment by regiment, they loaded the boats. The night was dark, the work dangerous. One wrong sound could alert the British. Washington refused to leave his post on the Brooklyn side, supervising the evacuation.

"Sir," an aide pleaded, "you must get some rest."

"I will rest," Washington replied grimly, "when the last man is across."

Sometime after midnight, the wind turned against them. The boats struggled against the current. Washington's heart sank. They needed more time.

Then, as if by divine providence, a thick fog rolled in, cloaking the operation in an impenetrable blanket of white.

Dawn broke over Long Island, and Howe prepared to begin his bombardment. But as the fog lifted, he stared in disbelief at the American fortifications.

Empty.

Nine thousand men, their artillery, their supplies—all gone, spirited away in the night.

"Impossible," he muttered. But the evidence was before his eyes. His prey had slipped away.

On the Manhattan side, Washington finally allowed himself to breathe. The last boat had landed just moments ago. An entire army, snatched from the jaws of defeat.

He clasped Glover's shoulder. "Colonel, you and your men have saved the Continental Army."

The fisherman shrugged modestly. "Just another night's work on the water, sir."

Washington smiled, but his eyes were grave. They had escaped disaster, but only just. The real test of this army - and its commander - still lay ahead.

Behind them, the fog finally lifted from the East River, revealing their miracle to the astonished British. But by then, it was too late. The Continental Army would live to fight another day.

In his first major battle, Washington had been outmaneuvered and nearly destroyed. But in defeat, he had learned perhaps his most valuable lesson: sometimes, knowing when to retreat was as important as knowing when to fight.

The war was far from over. But on this morning, that was enough..

Chapter 47

One Life to Give

New York City - September 22, 1776
Dawn

The first light of morning creeps through the window of my makeshift prison. Strange, how much sweeter the sunrise looks when you know it will be your last. I, Nathan Hale, aged twenty-one years, will not live to see it set.

They will hang me as a spy in a few hours. Captain Cunningham, that brute of a provost marshal, took particular pleasure in telling me so. No Bible to comfort me in my final hours, he said. No paper to write a last letter to my family. Let the rebel spy die without consolation.

Yet they cannot take my thoughts, and in these quiet moments before dawn, they turn to what brought me here.

"I wish to be useful." Those were my words when I volunteered for this mission. General Washington needed information about British positions in New York, and I stepped forward. My fellow officers tried to dissuade me. Teaching school in New London had hardly prepared me for the art of espionage, they said.

Perhaps they were right. A week of trying to gather intelligence while posing as a Dutch schoolmaster, only to be betrayed by my own cousin, Samuel Hale, if the rumors I've heard are true. What a poor spy I proved to be.

My thoughts drift to my classroom in New London, to eager young faces looking up at me as I expounded on Latin verbs and mathematics. How long ago that seems now, though it's been barely a year. I wonder if any of my students will remember their young teacher who died for the cause of liberty?

And Enoch, my dear brother. News of my death will hit him hardest. We shared everything growing up—games, studies at Yale, dreams for the future. "Be careful," he warned me when I joined the fight. "Your patriotic heart will lead you into danger." How prophetic his words proved to be.

The sounds of the awakening city drift through my window. Soon, they will come for me. I find my thoughts turning to Brutus, whose noble death I once taught my students about. He too died for the cause of liberty. There is comfort in that parallel, though I doubt my death will merit more than a footnote in history's pages.

Yet I do not regret my choice. Our cause is just, our need for liberty real. If my death serves that cause in some small way, then it has meaning.

Footsteps in the corridor. The door creaks open, and there stands Cunningham, his face twisted in its usual sneer.

"Time to go, rebel."

I stand, straightening my clothes as best I can. They had stripped me of my Continental Army uniform days ago, but they cannot strip me of my dignity.

As they lead me out into the morning air, I see the crowd already gathering. The British mean this to be a spectacle, a warning to other would-be spies. Very well. I shall give them a spectacle, but not the one they expect.

The walk to the gallows seems both eternally long and startlingly short. Each step brings memories: Mother reading to me from the

Bible, Father teaching me to ride, Professor Daggett's lectures at Yale, the faces of my students, the proud day I joined the fight for independence.

They ask if I have any last words.

Looking out at the assembled crowd, I speak clearly, my voice carrying on the morning air: *"I only regret that I have but one life to lose for my country."*

Let them remember that. Let them remember that a Yale scholar, a Connecticut schoolmaster, a son of liberty, went to his death not with fear or regret, but with devotion to a cause greater than himself.

The sun has fully risen now, painting the sky in brilliant hues. My last sunrise, and it is glorious. Perhaps, years from now, others will see such a sunrise and remember that men died so they could live free.

I close my eyes and think of home, of New England's green hills, of all that we fight for. One life seems a small price to pay for such a worthy cause.

They place the hood over my head. In the darkness, I whisper a final prayer:

"God of our fathers, grant that my sacrifice may serve the cause of liberty. Let future generations know that in America's darkest hour, her sons stood ready to give their all for her freedom."

The drum rolls. The trap door opens. My one life given for my country.

Let history judge if I gave it well.

[Historical note: Nathan Hale's execution took place on the morning of September 22, 1776. His famous last words have inspired generations of Americans, making him one of the Revolution's most memorable heroes. He was 21 years old.]

Chapter 48

A Kingdom's Burden

10 Downing Street, London - November 1776

I, Frederick North, Prime Minister of Great Britain, stood at my window watching a cold November rain fall on London's streets. On my desk lay the latest dispatches from America—a litany of problems that would require explanations to both Parliament and King.

Howe had taken New York, yes. But Washington's army had somehow slipped away. Again. The massive amphibious operation, the largest deployment of British forces ever attempted, had gained us...a city.

"My lord?" My secretary appeared at the door. "His Majesty requests your presence at St. James's Palace. This afternoon."

I nodded wearily. George would want to discuss the latest news, particularly this absurd "Declaration" the rebels had published. As if thirteen colonies could simply vote themselves out of the greatest empire on Earth.

Before attending the King, I had some time to collect my thoughts. Five years as Prime Minister, and never had I faced such a crisis. The American problem had seemed manageable at first.

A few shows of force, perhaps some diplomatic concessions, and surely the colonies would return to proper behavior.

How wrong we had been.

I picked up the latest fiscal report. The war was bleeding the treasury dry. Ships, supplies, mercenaries—none came cheaply. The opposition in Parliament grew stronger daily. Burke's speeches about conciliation found increasingly receptive ears.

"They're our own people," he had thundered in the Commons last week. "English blood flows in their veins!"

But they had rejected that blood tie, hadn't they? Their Declaration spoke of a "separate and equal station" among the powers of Earth. The very idea was preposterous. Yet...

I pulled out a report from one of our agents in Paris. The French were watching events with keen interest. Rumors spoke of secret meetings, of arms shipments, of possible alliance with the rebels. Surely they wouldn't dare. Yet the possibility haunted my nights.

The clock struck three. Time to face George.

At St. James's Palace, I found the King in an agitated state, pacing his chamber.

"North! Have you seen this latest outrage?" He thrust a paper at me—another copy of the Declaration. "They dare to list their grievances against me? Against their rightful sovereign?"

"Your Majesty, the document is mere propaganda-"

"They call me a tyrant, North! Me, who has only sought to govern them justly, to protect them, to-"

"Sire," I interrupted gently, "perhaps we might discuss our military situation?"

The King's face darkened. "Howe moves too slowly. The rebellion should have been crushed by now."

I chose my next words carefully. "The geography works against us, Your Majesty. Supply lines stretch across an ocean. The rebels fade into the countryside when pressed, only to reappear else-where. And winter approaches."

"Excuses!" George snapped. "I want this rebellion ended, North. Whatever the cost."

Whatever the cost. There was the rub. The cost already exceeded anything we had imagined. Not just in pounds sterling, but in lives, in relationships sundered, in the very fabric of empire torn asunder.

Later that evening, in my study, I penned notes for tomorrow's address to Parliament. They would want explanations, strategies, timelines. I had none to give them.

A knock at the door - more dispatches. I opened them without enthusiasm. Reports of unrest in Ireland. Spanish naval move-ments near Gibraltar. Dutch merchants trading with the rebels.

Was this how empires fell? Not with dramatic battles, but with the slow accumulation of problems, each manageable alone, but together...

I poured myself a glass of port. Across the ocean, Washington gathered what remained of his army. In Paris, Franklin charmed the French court. In London, my political enemies sharpened their knives.

And I, Frederick North, stood at the center of it all, trying to hold together an empire that seemed determined to fly apart.

The rain continued to fall outside my window. Somewhere in the darkness, a church bell tolled - a mournful sound, like a funeral knell.

For what, I wondered? For the rebellion? For the empire?

Or perhaps for the simple certainty we had all possessed, not so long ago, when the world had made sense and thirteen trouble-some colonies had still been firmly British.

Only time would tell. But as I turned back to my endless papers, I couldn't shake the feeling that we had passed a point of no return, and that all the King's horses and all the King's men might not be able to put this empire back together again.

Chapter 49

Victory or Death

Crossing the Delaware

Delaware River Camp - December 25, 1776

The wind howled through the Continental Army's camp as I, George Washington, read again the words that had stirred my soul: *"These are the times that try men's souls. The summer soldier and the sunshine patriot will, in this crisis, shrink from the service of their country..."*

Thomas Paine's new pamphlet spoke truth. After the disasters at New York, after months of retreat, my army was shrinking daily. Enlistments would expire in a week. If we didn't act now, there might not be an army left to command.

I set down the pamphlet and studied the map. Across the Delaware River, the Hessians at Trenton celebrated Christmas. Colonel Rall, their commander, had dismissed warnings of an American attack. His overconfidence would be his undoing—if we could cross the river.

"General?" Henry Knox entered my tent. "The men are ready."

"Very well," I nodded. "Ensure all units understand the challenge and countersign. We cannot risk confusion in the dark."

"'Victory' and 'Or Death', sir. Every commander has been informed."

How fitting those words were. It was indeed victory or death—not just for us, but for the cause of independence itself.

The crossing was a nightmare of cold and ice. From my position in the lead boat, I watched Glover's Marblehead men battle the elements. These fishermen, who had saved us at Brooklyn, were performing another miracle.

"Keep rowing!" Glover shouted above the storm. "The Commander-in-Chief is watching!"

Indeed I was, and my heart swelled with pride at their determination. The wind cut through my cloak, but I remained standing. The men needed to see their General sharing their hardship.

Hours behind schedule, we finally reached the far shore. No turning back now. Knox began moving the artillery up the bank—eighteen precious guns that would prove decisive.

"Form up!" I ordered. "We march on Trenton!"

The men, though exhausted from the crossing, moved with grim purpose. Nine miles to Trenton, through driving sleet. Every step was agony, their frozen rags offering little protection. Two men collapsed from the cold. I saw their bloodied footprints in the snow.

The column moved slowly through the frozen dark, each step a battle against exhaustion and the biting wind. Suddenly, shapes loomed ahead on the road. Men raised their muskets.

"Halt!" came a challenge from the shadows. "Who goes there?"

I reined in my horse, listening intently. This could be a Hessian patrol—or our own advance guard.

"Victory!" called out Colonel Hand, commander of our forward unit.

"Or Death!" came the response.

The tension eased as the shapes materialized into Knox's artillery unit, struggling to move the heavy guns through the snow. The password had served its purpose—friendly forces had identified each other without giving away our position to the enemy.

Throughout the nine-mile march, this scene would repeat itself. "Victory!" "Or Death!" Each exchange a reminder of what was at stake. We had chosen these words deliberately—there would be no middle ground tonight. We would either achieve a victory that would resurrect our cause, or we would meet our death in the attempt.

Dawn was breaking as we approached Trenton. We were hours late—the surprise attack should have happened in darkness. Had we lost our chance?

Then salvation—the storm had delayed the Hessian patrols as well. Their guard was still light, their garrison still sleeping off Christmas celebrations.

"Attack!" I ordered, my voice carrying over the storm. "Long live liberty!"

Knox's artillery opened up, catching the Hessians completely by surprise. I spurred my horse forward, sword drawn. This was no time for a general to command from the rear.

The battle was swift and decisive. Rall tried to rally his men, but our trap was perfect. Within an hour, it was over. Nearly nine hundred prisoners, tons of supplies, and most importantly – victory.

But there was no time to rest. The enemy would respond. An idea formed—why not strike again?

"Knox!" I called. "Can the men manage another march?"

His grin told me all I needed to know.

Two days later, we slipped away from Trenton in the night, leaving our campfires burning to fool Cornwallis. By dawn, we were approaching Princeton.

The resulting battle nearly ended in disaster. Our vanguard retreated in disorder. I rode forward, directly between the lines.

"Halt!" I shouted. "Rally behind me!"

For a moment, time seemed to stop. Later, soldiers swore I was untouchable as bullets whizzed past. The men rallied. We attacked. Princeton fell.

Now, a week after crossing the Delaware, I sit in my tent writing to Congress. Two victories had changed everything. Enlistments were up. The army's spirit was restored. The cause of independence had new life.

On my desk lay Paine's pamphlet, open to its stirring words: "The harder the conflict, the more glorious the triumph."

We had earned that glory, paid for it with frozen feet and desperate courage. But more importantly, we had shown that the Continental Army could not only survive, but win.

The war was far from over. But on this winter's night, as my exhausted men celebrated our victories, I allowed myself a moment of satisfaction. Our password had been "Victory" and "Or Death."

We had chosen Victory.

Chapter 50

The Cost of Empire

London - March 1777

I, William Hardcastle, merchant of London and partner in Hardcastle & Sons Trading Company, stared at the ledger before me. The columns of figures told a grim tale—one that neither Parliament nor the King seemed to fully grasp.

Three generations of Hardcastles had built this business. My grandfather had established our first connections in Boston. My father had expanded to Philadelphia, Charleston, and beyond. And I? I was watching it all unravel.

"Another ship lost, sir." Thomas, my clerk, laid a report on my desk. "The Fair Caroline. Taken by rebel privateers off the Carolina coast."

I closed my eyes, picturing the cargo manifest. Cotton, indigo, tobacco - all gone. And more importantly, the web of relationships, of trust and credit, built over decades.

Opening my desk drawer, I withdrew letters from my former business partners in America. John Adams in Boston—now some sort of rebel leader. William Morris in Philadelphia—financing their so-called Continental Congress. Even loyal old James Brighton in Charleston had reluctantly closed our accounts.

"Understand, William," Brighton had written, "it's not just the boycotts or the Committees of Correspondence watching our every move. Things have changed. We're becoming something different here—no longer just British subjects trading with the mother country."

A knock at my office door interrupted my brooding. "Enter!"

My son Edward, recently returned from our Bristol office, strode in. "Father, we need to talk about the American trade."

"What's left of it," I muttered.

"Exactly. Our ships can't get into most colonial ports. When they do, they risk capture by rebels. Insurance rates have tripled. And now, after Washington's victories at Trenton and Princeton ..."

"Don't remind me," I growled. Those battles had done more than boost rebel morale—they'd convinced many merchants that reconciliation was increasingly unlikely.

Edward pressed on. "We need to shift our focus. The Mediterranean trade, perhaps. Or the East Indies."

"Your grandfather would roll in his grave. The American trade was our foundation!"

"Was, Father. Was." Edward's voice softened. "Times change. The colonies...they're not colonies anymore, are they?"

I stood and walked to the window, looking out over the Thames. Ships still crowded the river, but something was different. The familiar sight of American trading vessels, their holds full of tobacco, rice, and timber, had vanished.

"Did you know," I said quietly, "that I apprenticed in Boston? Lived with the Adams family for a year. John was just a boy then. Now he signs declarations calling our King a tyrant."

"All the more reason to adapt," Edward urged. "Other houses are already doing it. Harrison & Company has shifted entirely to India. The Jameson brothers are focusing on the Caribbean."

I picked up the latest newspaper. More debates in Parliament about the cost of the war. More calls for harsh measures against the rebels. More ships and troops being sent across the Atlantic.

"They don't understand," I murmured.

"Who doesn't?"

"Parliament. The King. They see this as a rebellion to be crushed. They don't see that we're losing something precious—not just taxes or authority, but relationships. Trust. Understanding."

I pulled out our company's first ledger, kept by my grandfather. The names leapt out at me—Adams, Hancock, Morris, Rutledge. All rebel names now.

"We didn't just trade goods," I said. "We traded ideas, culture, friendship. Every ship that sailed strengthened the bonds between us. Now..."

"Now we adapt," Edward said firmly. "The world is changing, Father. We can change with it, or we can cling to the past and sink."

He was right, of course. The boy had better business sense than his sentimental old father. But as I looked at the pile of letters, the ledgers showing mounting losses, the news of battles and declarations, I mourned for something more than just profits.

I mourned for the loss of a relationship between peoples that had once seemed as natural as breathing. For the trust built over generations, shattered by pride and misunderstanding on both sides.

"Very well," I sighed. "Draw up proposals for new trading routes. But keep our American factors on the books, just in case..."

Edward nodded, though we both knew it was a futile gesture. There would be no going back to the way things were.

As my son left to begin our company's transformation, I found myself remembering a line from Brighton's letter: "We're becoming something different here."

Indeed they were. And so, I realized, were we all.

Chapter 51

A Government in Flight

Congress Flees Philadelphia, Sept. 1777

Philadelphia, September 18, 1777

The Continental Congress dissolves in chaos as I, John Adams, stuff vital papers into my saddlebags. Outside, church bells toll in alarm—the British are approaching Philadelphia. Brandywine Creek has been lost, and with it, our ability to defend the capital.

"Mr. Adams!" Charles Thomson, our harried secretary, rushes past with an armful of documents. "What of the Declaration? The Articles of Confederation draft?"

"Safe," I assure him. "I've entrusted them to special couriers. They ride for Lancaster."

The scene before me is one I never imagined when we boldly declared independence fourteen months ago. The Continental Congress—the government of our fledgling nation—reduced to a panicked evacuation.

"Mr. Adams!" Young James Lovell appears at my elbow. "Word from the militia—British advance units are less than ten miles distant."

I nod grimly. How quickly circumstances change. Just days ago, we were confident Washington could hold them at Brandywine. Now...

The crack of a wheel breaking draws my attention. One of the wagons, overloaded with congressional records, has foundered in the street. Thomson looks ready to weep as clerks scramble to gather scattered papers.

"Leave the routine correspondence!" I shout. "Save the vital documents—military communications, diplomatic papers, treasury records!"

My mind races with the implications of this retreat. What will it mean for the cause of independence when word spreads that Congress has fled its own capital? How will it affect our negotiations with France?

A courier arrives with a dispatch from Washington. I read it quickly—his army is regrouping, but cannot prevent Howe from taking Philadelphia. The city is lost.

"Lancaster!" someone calls out. "Congress will reconvene in Lancaster!"

But for how long? Lancaster may not be far enough. Some are already suggesting York, further west.

As I mount my horse, I catch sight of my lodging house where I've spent so many months. The good widow who runs it stands in the doorway, tears in her eyes. This is harder for the civilians—they cannot flee with us.

"Keep faith, madam," I call to her. "We shall return."

Will we? The question haunts me as our ragged procession moves through the streets. Delegates on horseback, wagons loaded with documents, clerks and servants on foot—the government of the United States reduced to a band of refugees.

I think of Abigail, safe in Braintree. What would she make of this scene? Her last letter urged perseverance: "Though we have been disappointed in our hopes, we should not despair."

Easy to write from Massachusetts. Harder to believe as I watch the largest city in the colonies slip from our grasp.

Yet as we clear Philadelphia's outskirts, I notice something remarkable. Despite the chaos, despite the fear, the machinery of government continues to function. Thomson protects his precious records. Delegates discuss plans for the next session. Committees meet on horseback.

We are learning, perhaps, that a government need not be bound to a single place. Like our army, we can retreat, regroup, and carry on the fight.

The sun sets behind us as we ride west, casting long shadows on the road to Lancaster. Philadelphia may fall to the British, but they cannot capture the idea of independence, the spirit of liberty that drives us forward.

I reach into my coat and touch a letter from Benjamin Franklin in Paris. His words come back to me: "Indeed, we have nothing to fear but our own divisions."

Tonight, at least, we remain united—if only in flight. Tomorrow, from Lancaster or York or wherever fate drives us, we will continue our work. The British may take our capital, but they cannot take our resolve.

As darkness falls, I look back one last time at Philadelphia's distant spires. We will return, I vow silently. And when we do, it will be as representatives not of thirteen rebellious colonies, but of a free and independent nation.

For now, though, we ride west, a Congress in exile, carrying with us the dream of America.

Chapter 52

Fortune's Wheel

The Battle of Saratoga, Oct. 1777

Saratoga - October 1777

General Horatio Gates:

History, I muse, watching the enemy lines through my spyglass, has a delicious sense of irony. Here stands "Gentleman Johnny" Burgoyne, the most sophisticated general in the British Army, trapped by colonial forces in the wilderness he so disdained.

And here stand I, Horatio Gates, to receive his surrender. Not Washington, with his Virginia plantation manners. Not that popinjay Arnold, currently nursing his wounds and his wounded pride. But I, the professional soldier who has argued all along for proper military tactics rather than Washington's constant retreats.

"Sir?" My aide interrupts my thoughts. "General Arnold is demanding to lead another attack."

I wave him away in irritation. Arnold - always Arnold. The man fought brilliantly, I'll grant him that, but his reckless charges at Bemis Heights could have cost us everything. Now he lies wounded, still trying to steal my glory.

"Tell General Arnold that his services are no longer required." The words taste sweet. "The enemy is finished."

Indeed they are. Burgoyne's army is surrounded, starving, their Native American allies long fled. My strategy of patience has paid off. While Washington loses Philadelphia, I have caught and will destroy an entire British army.

A messenger arrives with congratulations from Congress. I can almost taste their relief at finally having a commanding general who can deliver victory. Washington, for all his dignity, has given them nothing but retreats and defeats.

Perhaps, I reflect, it is time for a change in overall command...

The next day dawns bright and clear—perfect weather for a surrender ceremony. I have arranged everything carefully. Burgoyne, I hear, is particular about military protocol. Very well, let him have his dignity. It will only enhance the magnitude of our triumph.

As I prepare to receive the surrender, I pen a quick note to Congress. No need to send this victory report through Washington. After all, this is my victory, my moment. And perhaps, soon, my army.

I smile as I mount my horse. Today, Horatio Gates enters history.

Private William Jameson, 9th Regiment of Foot:

They're making us stack arms in formation, a final parade before our shame is complete. General Burgoyne, resplendent in his best uniform, looks like he's attending a London social gathering rather than a surrender.

The Americans line both sides of the road—thousands of them, more than I imagined existed in this godforsaken wilderness. They're not the rabble we were told to expect. Their lines are straight, their weapons well-maintained. They look like soldiers.

"Eyes front," our sergeant hisses. We're to march out with dignity, he says. Show these colonials that British regulars know how to comport themselves, even in defeat.

But it's hard to maintain dignity when your stomach is cramping from weeks of short rations. When you've watched half your mates die in this endless forest. When you're surrendering to men you were told were inferior in every way.

Their General Gates sits his horse like a proper officer. Behind him stands a harder-looking lot—frontier fighters who taught us the meaning of fear in these woods. One of them, they say, is Benedict Arnold, the devil himself by our officers' telling. He took a ball in the leg but still kept fighting.

The fifes play "The World Turned Upside Down" as we march between the American lines. Someone in their ranks calls out, "Welcome to the Republic!" A few men laugh, but there's no real mockery in it. They know what it is to be soldiers.

Burgoyne hands over his sword with a flourish. More theater, but I suppose it helps him bear it. The Americans present arms smartly—a soldier's salute to soldiers, even beaten ones.

As I lay my Brown Bess in the growing pile of surrendered weapons, I catch the eye of an American militiaman about my age. There's no triumph in his look, just a weary acknowledgment. We're both soldiers, doing what soldiers do.

Later, sharing surprisingly generous American rations, we learn that Gates has granted us "the Honors of War"—respect for defeated brothers-in-arms. It helps, a little. So does the American coffee, bitter but hot.

Tonight, by the campfire, an American sergeant tells us we'll be marched to Boston, then probably shipped home. "No parole," he says apologetically. "Can't risk you joining Howe's army."

Smart, that. These Americans have learned soldiering faster than anyone thought possible. I touch the spot where my cartridge box used to hang and wonder what they're saying in London tonight. Do they know yet that an entire British army has been lost? That these "colonies" have become something else—something that can defeat Europe's best troops in open battle?

The Americans have posted guards, but they're not watching us very closely. They know we're done fighting. Besides, where would we go in this vast land that has swallowed us?

Tomorrow we begin the march to Boston. Some of the lads talk about returning with a bigger army, but I hear doubt in their voices. Something has changed here in the wilderness of Saratoga. The world truly has turned upside down.

I save a piece of hardtack from our surrender rations. Something to show my grandchildren someday, when they ask about the war in America. "This," I'll tell them, "is from the day we learned the colonies weren't colonies anymore."

Chapter 53

The Forging

Valley Forge, Winter 1777-1778

I am Winter, and I have seen many wars. I watched Hannibal cross the Alps, Napoleon retreat from Moscow, armies clash and kings fall. But never have I witnessed anything quite like Valley Forge.

They arrived in December, these ragged Continentals, more mob than army. Their shoes were gone, their clothes thin and torn. I tried, in those first days, to hold back my chill winds, to let them build their huts, to give them time.

But I am Winter. I cannot change my nature.

The first storm came just before Christmas. I watched young Private Williams, barely sixteen, try to warm his bare feet by a dying fire. His toes were already black with frostbite. He wouldn't last the month. I wrapped him in soft snow when the end came, a blanket of white to ease his passing.

"Don't cry, mother," he whispered to the darkness. "I died for freedom."

The cold grew deeper. In the officers' huts, I heard Washington's prayers each night. "God help us endure," he would murmur, and

I wanted to answer, to tell him that endurance comes at a terrible price.

I saw soldiers boiling their leather straps for soup, watched them leave bloody footprints in my snow as they foraged for firewood. Each morning brought more bodies, frozen in the night. I covered them gently, respectfully. They had earned that much.

But something strange began to happen. Those who survived grew stronger. A Prussian arrived - von Steuben - cursing magnificently in three languages as he drilled them in the snow. I helped sometimes, calming my winds so his voice would carry across the parade ground.

"Again!" he would shout. "Again, you wonderful peasants! Show the world what you can become!"

And they did. Day by day, drill by drill, they transformed. My ice coated their muskets, but they learned to care for them. My winds howled through their formations, but they held their lines. My frost bit at their flesh, but they endured.

I watched Timothy Cooper, a Massachusetts farmer, share his last crust of bread with a Virginia gentleman. In my world of white, the divisions between them melted away. They were becoming something new—not just an army, but Americans.

Some nights, I would ease the bitter cold, let them gather around their fires to sing and tell stories. I listened with them, heard tales of homes left behind, of dreams of liberty, of a future they might never see but believed in enough to die for.

Sarah arrived in January, one of the camp followers who kept these men alive. She had walked three days through my deepest drifts to bring her husband a pair of boots. I gentled the storm that night, gave them one evening together before pneumonia took her. He survived, wearing the boots she died bringing him, and I heard him whisper "thank you" to her memory with each step.

February brought the worst cold, but also hope. Supply lines finally opened. Food arrived. New uniforms. But by then, these men didn't need them to stand tall. They had found something stronger than comfort, more sustaining than food.

I am Winter. I have frozen oceans and buried cities. But I could not break these men. Instead, I watched as they were forged into steel, tempered by suffering, strengthened by sacrifice.

When spring finally came, I lingered longer than usual, unwilling to leave. The army that marched out of Valley Forge was not the one that had stumbled in. They had become warriors, brothers, a force that would win a nation's freedom.

Years later, those who survived would tell their grandchildren about that winter. They would speak of the cold, the hunger, the death. But also of the transformation, the brotherhood, the birth of an army and a nation.

And I, Winter, who watched it all, who wrapped the dead in white shrouds and challenged the living with my bitter winds, I remember too. I remember every frozen tear, every act of kindness, every dawn that found them still standing, still defiant.

I am Winter. I have seen empires rise and fall. But I have never been prouder than when I tested these men and found them equal to their dream of freedom.

They named a place for me - Valley Forge - where winter helped birth a nation. It is a worthy monument, not to my power to destroy, but to humanity's capacity to endure, to transform, to emerge stronger from the deepest cold.

Remember them. Remember that winter. And know that sometimes, the hardest seasons forge the strongest souls.

Chapter 54

Franklin's Game

The Treaty with France, Feb. 1778

Paris - February 6, 1778

I, Benjamin Franklin, adjust my plain brown suit and set my beaver fur cap just so. The French courtiers will expect "le bon Franklin" to play his role—the simple American sage amid Versailles splendor. Very well. Let them smile at my rustic appearance. Today, their smiles will sign a treaty.

"Dr. Franklin?" My secretary appears at the door. "Your carriage awaits."

I nod, suppressing a smile. If they only knew how deliberately I have orchestrated every detail of this grand performance. For two years, I have played on French expectations, hopes, and vanities. The plain dress, the spectacles, the homespun wisdom—all calculated to charm a society drowning in artifice.

"Be seen at the right salons," I had written to Congress. "Charm the ladies. Let them think they are discovering America's virtues for themselves."

As my carriage winds through Paris streets, I reflect on the long game that has led to this day. When I first arrived, France was interested but cautious. They enjoyed needling Britain but feared committing to our cause. "Show us you can fight," they said, "and then we'll talk."

Well, Gates had shown them at Saratoga. An entire British army surrendered! The news hit Paris like a thunderbolt. Suddenly, those who had kept me at arm's length were eager to negotiate.

I pause at the entrance to the foreign ministry, remembering other negotiations in this building. Vergennes had been clever, probing for weakness, looking for advantage. But I had played my own game—letting slip rumors of British peace offers, hinting at reconciliation if France delayed too long.

"L'Amérique," I had told them, "is like a ripe fruit, ready to fall. The only question is, into whose basket?"

Inside, the treaty documents await. I have read every word, debated every clause. France will declare war on Britain, provide arms, money, and men. In return, we promise not to make a separate peace. A steep price, perhaps, but revolutions do not come cheaply.

"Ah, Dr. Franklin!" Vergennes approaches, elegant as always. "I trust you find the terms satisfactory?"

"As satisfactory as they are necessary, Your Excellency."

He smiles, appreciating the nuance. We both know this is more than a treaty—it is France's revenge for 1763, Britain's humiliation, and America's lifeline, all bound together in diplomatic language.

As we take our seats at the great table, I think of the parties at my house in Passy, where so much of this was really negotiated. The intellectual discussions that were really policy debates. The chess games that mirrored our diplomatic maneuvers. The flirtations with French ladies that carried messages more significant than mere gallantry.

"You play your role so well," the Countess de Noailles had said one evening. "The philosopher-pioneer, charming us with simplicity."

"My dear Countess," I had replied, "is it a role if one believes in it?"

The scratching of quills brings me back to the present. Names are being signed, seals affixed. Vergennes hands me the pen with a flourish.

As I sign, I think of Valley Forge, where Washington's army shivers in the snow. Of battles fought with too few guns, too little powder. That ends today. France's mighty arms industry will now supply our cause. Her navy will challenge British control of the seas.

"It is done," Vergennes announces. Champagne appears, toasts are made.

"To freedom," I offer, raising my glass.

"To alliance," Vergennes responds.

To necessity, I think but do not say. France needs to weaken Britain. We need French aid. A marriage of convenience, perhaps, but no less significant for that.

Later, riding home to Passy, I pen a quick note to Congress. "The treaty is signed. America now has a powerful friend."

I pause, considering what to add. Should I explain how many dinners, how many witty remarks, how many carefully calculated gestures it took to reach this day? How I played on French philosophical pretensions and anti-British sentiment? How I turned my age and reputation into diplomatic weapons?

No. Let history wonder how the plainest man in Paris accomplished the most elaborate diplomatic triumph of the age. Tonight, I will play chess with the Duchess d'Enville, discuss electricity with the Academy of Sciences, and continue charming France into war with Britain.

All while wearing my plain brown suit and beaver hat. Sometimes, I reflect, the best diplomacy is simply knowing which role to play.

And I, Benjamin Franklin, have given the performance of my life.

Chapter 55
British Army Quits Philadelphia

THE PENNSYLVANIA GAZETTE
June 25, 1778

PHILADELPHIA - Our city awakens to a strange quiet following the departure of British forces under Sir Henry Clinton. After nine months of occupation, the streets that recently echoed with British drums now resound with the footsteps of returning patriots.

The British withdrawal, commencing June 18th, presented a spectacle unprecedented in our city's history. A column stretching nearly twelve miles departed via the Market Street ferry, carrying not only Clinton's army but also some three thousand Loyalist civilians who chose exile over facing their fellow Americans.

"The baggage train alone was a sight to behold," reports Mr. James Wilson, a merchant who observed the exodus. "Wagons loaded with the spoils of occupation—including, one suspects, much property belonging to our own citizens."

Sources confirm that General Washington, having crossed the Delaware with the Continental Army, pursues the British column across New Jersey. Our army, much transformed from the ragged force that retreated from New York two years ago, now hunts its former hunters.

The transition of power within Philadelphia has proceeded with remarkable order, thanks to the swift actions of General Benedict Arnold, appointed military commander of the city. Several suspected collaborators have been arrested, though Arnold urges restraint in dealing with those who cooperated with the occupation.

"Let us show the world," Arnold proclaimed, "that we can govern with justice, not vengeance."

Congress is expected to return within weeks, restoring Philadelphia as the capital of our revolution. Meanwhile, merchants report severe shortages of basic goods, the British having stripped the city's warehouses before departing.

More troubling are reports of damage to public buildings. The State House, while intact, shows evidence of British troops having used its interior woodwork for firewood during the winter. Several churches converted to hospitals require extensive repairs.

Yet amid these difficulties, citizens celebrate their liberation. "The British came as conquerors," observes Rev. William White, "but depart as fugitives, fleeing across New Jersey with Washington at their heels."

Indeed, preliminary reports indicate that General Washington's forces harass the British column daily. A major engagement appears imminent, perhaps near Monmouth Court House.

As Philadelphia recovers its liberty, one fact becomes clear: the British, who entered our city in triumph last September, leave it in what amounts to retreat. The cause of independence, tested but unbroken, lives on in its first capital.

[Further reports of military developments will be published as information arrives from New Jersey.]

NOTICES:

- Citizens who can prove theft or damage of property during the occupation may register claims at the State House.

- The Committee of Safety will meet tomorrow to discuss restoration of civil government.

- A prayer service of thanksgiving will be held Sunday at Christ Church.

[Price: Six Pence].

Chapter 56

More Than Water

The Battle of Monmouth, June 1778

Monmouth Court House, New Jersey - June 28, 1778

The sun rises like a hammer, promising heat that will forge this day in blood and fire. I, Mary Ludwig Hays—though the soldiers call me "Molly Pitcher"—begin my morning rounds with water for the artillery crews. My husband, John Hays, tends his cannon with the same care other men show their prized horses.

"Molly!" voices call out as I make my way through the lines. "Water!" The men's gratitude shows in their eyes—they know this day will be brutal. Even at dawn, the air shimmers with heat.

General Lee leads the advance force ahead of us. The main army under General Washington follows. We are hunting the British as they retreat across New Jersey, loaded down with their plunder from Philadelphia.

By midmorning, the heat is unbearable. My water bucket empties faster than I can fill it. Men collapse from sunstroke even before the fighting starts. Then, suddenly, confusion ripples through the ranks. Lee's men are falling back—no, retreating in disorder.

"What's happening?" John asks, peering through the dust cloud.

I've just returned from the spring when I see him—General Washington, riding toward the sound of gunfire, his face dark with fury. Never have I seen such controlled rage.

"What is the meaning of this?" his voice carries across the field. Lee stammers excuses.

The next hours blur into a haze of heat and gun smoke. Washington rallies the men, turns retreat into advance. The roar of cannon drowns out everything else. Back and forth I run with my water bucket, stepping over fallen men, dodging spent balls.

"Keep the guns firing!" officers shout. "Pour it to them!"

And we do, though the heat grows so intense that men touch the cannons at their peril. I see soldiers collapse, their faces red not from battle but from the murderous sun. My water now goes as much to cooling the guns as to cooling parched throats.

Then it happens. John falls, overcome by heat or worse—in the chaos, I cannot tell. But his gun falls silent, and in battle, a silent gun means death for others who depend on its fire.

I don't remember deciding. One moment I'm kneeling beside John, the next I'm at his position, ramming home the charge. The motions come naturally—I've watched him do this hundreds of times.

"Fire!" I hear myself shout, and the cannon roars to life.

Time loses meaning. Load, fire, reload. The British press their attack, fall back, attack again. My dress is black with powder, my face streaked with sweat and grime. The other gunners no longer stare—I'm just another soldier now, doing what must be done.

A British shot tears through my skirt. "That could have been worse," I mutter, ramming home another charge. The men nearby laugh—a strange sound in this hell of heat and death.

Later—hours? minutes?—I hear cheers rolling down the line. The British are withdrawing. We've held our ground. More than that—we've proven that the Continental Army can stand toe-to-toe with the King's best troops.

As evening approaches, bringing blessed relief from the heat, General Washington himself rides past our position. He stops, looking at me with my blackened dress and powder-stained face.

"Who is she?" I hear him ask.

"Molly Pitcher, sir," someone answers. "She worked her husband's gun when he fell."

Washington nods, a rare smile crossing his face. "Sergeant Molly," he says. "A fine name for a brave woman."

Later, I learn that John will recover—heat exhaustion, not a wound, had felled him. As I tend to him, I overhear officers discussing the battle. General Lee is under arrest for his retreat. The British have slipped away in the night. The day is counted a draw, or perhaps a small victory.

But I know something else happened here. The Continental Army proved itself equal to the British. And a woman proved herself equal to the task of combat. Both, perhaps, were inevitable—a new nation being born cannot be bound by old constraints.

I still carry water—that need does not end. But now the men look at me differently. "Sergeant Molly," they call me, and the respect in their voices has nothing to do with water.

They say this war is about liberty. Perhaps it's about more than just liberty from Britain. Perhaps it's about freedom to be more than others think we can be—whether that's colonies breaking from their king, or a woman doing what must be done on a battlefield.

As night falls over Monmouth battlefield, I clean John's gun one last time. Tomorrow we'll march again, following the British across New Jersey. And I'll be there, with my water bucket and, if needed, with the skill to do whatever else must be done.

For now, they call me Molly Pitcher. But I am more than that. Like this army, like this nation, I have proved myself capable of things once thought impossible.

And that, perhaps, is the real victory of Monmouth.

Chapter 57

A Change of Strategy

The Southern Campaign

New York City - December 15, 1778

To: Lord George Germain
Secretary of State for the Colonies
Whitehall, London

My Lord,

I write to propose a significant shift in our approach to subduing the rebellion. Events of the past year—the evacuation of Philadelphia, the indecisive engagement at Monmouth, and most crucially, the French entry into the war—demand a fresh strategy.

Our efforts in the northern colonies have reached a stalemate. Washington's army, while unable to drive us from New York, has grown increasingly professional. The French alliance provides them naval support that compromises our ability to operate freely along the coast. Moreover, the New England and mid-Atlantic colonies have proven stubbornly resistant to reconciliation.

However, the southern colonies present a more promising theater. Our intelligence suggests a strong Loyalist presence, particularly among the wealthy plantation owners. These men have much to lose from continued rebellion and much to gain from a return to Crown authority. Recent communications from South Carolina indicate that many await only the appearance of British forces to declare their loyalty openly.

The South also offers significant strategic advantages. The numerous deep harbors and navigable rivers will allow our navy to support land operations effectively. The capture of major ports—Savannah, Charleston, Wilmington—would sever the rebels' trading routes and deny them vital supplies.

Furthermore, the plantation economy of the South, particularly rice and tobacco, provides much of the rebels' hard currency through foreign trade. Controlling these resources would deal a severe blow to their ability to maintain their army and service their debts to France.

I propose to begin with Georgia, the weakest of the southern colonies. Savannah would make an excellent base of operations, allowing us to move northward into the Carolinas. As each area is secured, we can raise and arm Loyalist militias to maintain control, freeing our regulars to press forward.

This strategy offers several advantages:

1. Better utilization of our naval supremacy

2. Opportunity to rally substantial Loyalist support

3. Disruption of rebel commerce and supply lines

4. More favorable terrain for conventional military operations

5. Potential to isolate and defeat the southern rebel armies in detail

I have instructed Lieutenant Colonel Archibald Campbell to prepare an expedition against Savannah. With your approval, this will mark the beginning of our southern campaign.

There are, I must acknowledge, certain risks. The climate is harsh, particularly for European troops. Disease may prove as formidable an enemy as the rebels. Additionally, should the Loyalists prove less numerous or less committed than we hope, maintaining control of conquered territory could strain our limited forces.

Nevertheless, I believe this approach offers our best chance of success. The rebellion is like a structure—we have hammered at its roof in New England and its walls in the middle colonies. Perhaps it is time to attack its foundation in the South.

General Cornwallis has expressed enthusiasm for this strategy and would be my choice to lead the main thrust into the Carolinas once Georgia is secured. His aggressive nature and tactical skill make him well-suited for this role.

I await your thoughts on this proposal. Time is of the essence—the longer we delay, the more opportunity Washington and the French have to strengthen their position in the North.

Your most humble and obedient servant,

Henry Clinton
Commander-in-Chief, North America

P.S. - Early reports indicate Campbell's expedition has already seized Savannah. This initial success augurs well for our southern strategy.

Chapter 58

Not Yet Begun to Fight

John Paul Jones and HMS Serapis

Off Flamborough Head, England - September 23, 1779

The setting sun paints the North Sea crimson as I, John Paul Jones, guide the Bonhomme Richard toward our prey. From humble beginnings as a Scottish merchant sailor, I now command an American warship off the British coast. Life takes strange turns—I once fled these waters after a mutinous crew member died under my command. Now I return as a hunter.

HMS Serapis is magnificent—forty-four guns to our forty-two, but hers are newer, uniform, reliable. My guns are a mongrel collection, some ancient, some suspect. Like my crew—Americans, French, Portuguese, even some British—we're a makeshift force carrying the hopes of a makeshift navy.

"She's turning to engage, Captain!" my lookout calls.

Perfect. Let them come. My French-built ship might be old, but my American spirit burns fierce. Three years of commerce raiding have taught us our craft. We've terrorized British shipping, shown them that their former colonies can strike at their maritime heart.

But this...this will be different. A full broadside engagement with one of His Majesty's finest frigates.

The first broadside from Serapis tears into us like a giant's fist. Several of our old guns explode, killing their own crews. Through the smoke, I see splintered wood, broken bodies, the beginning of what will be a long night.

"Return fire!" I command, my voice carrying over the chaos.

The ships draw closer, trading broadsides in the gathering dark. Each exchange shows the disparity in our armament. Their gun crews are professional, their shots precise. We compensate with fury and determination.

Then disaster—a full broadside from Serapis tears into our hull below the waterline. The old timber splits like kindling.

"Captain!" my first officer shouts. "We're taking on water! The pumps can't keep up!"

Through the smoke, I hear Captain Pearson of the Serapis call out: "Has your ship struck?"

Struck our colors? Surrendered? I think of Congress's faith in giving me this command, of Benjamin Franklin's support in Paris, of all we're fighting to build. With my voice carrying clearly across the water, I reply: *"I have not yet begun to fight!"*

My crew roars in approval. We're Americans now, all of us, no matter where we were born. And Americans don't surrender.

I order the helmsman to ram Serapis. If we can't match her gun-for-gun, we'll board her. The ships collide with a sound like thunder, our rigging entangling. Now we're locked in a deadly embrace, so close our gun muzzles touch.

"Prepare to board!" I shout. But the British are ready. Grenades and musket fire rake our decks. Below, I can hear the growing slosh of water in our hold. The Bonhomme Richard is dying, but by God, she'll take Serapis with her.

For three hours we fight in the dark, the ships grinding against each other like massive sea beasts locked in combat. Our maintop sharpshooters rain fire down on Serapis's deck while below, our marines repel British boarding parties. The sea runs red with blood from both crews.

I see young Thomas Johnson, a Massachusetts boy of seventeen, rally his gun crew even with splinters as big as dock planks embedded in his shoulder. Old Miguel, our Portuguese carpenter, leads a party fighting the endless leaks below. Every man gives everything.

Then fate intervenes. One of our sailors, crawling out along the yardarm, drops a grenade down Serapis's main hatch. The explosion rips through their gun deck, silencing half their batteries at once. This is our moment.

"Board her!" I command, leading the charge myself. The fighting is savage—cutlass against cutlass, pistol against pistol, hatred against desperation. But we've done it. Captain Pearson himself hands me his sword.

Only then do I fully realize our condition. The Bonhomme Richard is finished, barely afloat. We've won the battle but lost our ship. The next morning, we transfer to Serapis as our faithful vessel slips beneath the waves, her American colors still flying.

But we've done what we set out to do. We've shown Britain that America can fight at sea. We've brought the war to their very doorstep. Most importantly, we've shown what determination can accomplish against superior force.

Looking back at the sinking Bonhomme Richard, I reflect on my journey—from Scottish merchant sailor to American captain. Like my adopted country, I've seized my destiny through sheer determination. The ship may be gone, but the spirit that fought her lives on.

They'll tell tales of this battle, I think. Perhaps they'll remember my words about not yet beginning to fight. But what I hope they remember most is this: America is now a sea power. We've proved it here, off Flamborough Head, in sight of the English shore.

Later, in my cabin aboard Serapis, I write in my log: "The mission is accomplished—not exactly as we planned, but in a way that will teach the world that America means to control its own destiny."

As we set sail for France in our captured prize, I order the American flag raised high. Let all who see it know—the colonies they dismissed as mere rabble have built a navy that can challenge the greatest maritime power on Earth.

We have, indeed, only begun to fight.

Chapter 59

A Matter of Training
The Battle of Camden

Camden, South Carolina - August 16, 1780

I, Joshua Cooper of the South Carolina militia, will never forget the morning our army broke. We had marched through the night, stomachs empty, legs weary. Most of us had been living on green corn and unripe peaches—General Gates seemed more concerned with speed than feeding his men.

"We outnumber them," the regulars kept telling us. "Almost two to one."

Numbers. As if numbers alone made an army.

Dawn was breaking when we heard the British drums. Through the morning mist, we saw them forming their lines—red coats brilliant in the growing light. Professional soldiers, every one of them. I looked at my own companions—farmers, craftsmen, shopkeepers. Many had never fired a musket in anger.

"Form up!" came the orders. They placed us militia on the left, Virginia militia beside us. The Continental regulars, including General de Kalb's men, formed our right. A proper battle line, just like Gates wanted.

The first British volley crashed out. Men fell. We responded raggedly, some of us forgetting to load in our nervousness. Then came the command we dreaded:

"Bayonets!"

The British line advanced, sunlight glinting off their wall of steel. We militia had few bayonets. Some men carried hunting rifles that couldn't mount them at all.

Someone screamed. Our line wavered. The British were getting closer, moving with the precision of long practice. Beside me, Thomas Williams threw down his musket and ran. Then another man. And another.

"Stand fast!" our officers shouted. But it was too late.

I'd like to say I stood my ground. I'd like to say I fought bravely. But when I saw that steel wall approaching, my courage failed. I ran, like hundreds of others. The shame of that moment burns me still.

Behind us, we could hear the Continental regulars fighting on. De Kalb's men stood their ground, fighting with desperate courage. We militia, who had boasted the night before about what we would do to the British, left them to die.

I ran until my lungs burned. Others ran further—some, they say, didn't stop until they reached North Carolina. General Gates himself galloped past us, riding hard for the horizon. The hero of Saratoga, fleeing the field at Camden.

Later, we learned the full extent of the disaster. De Kalb mortally wounded. A thousand men captured. Our army shattered. The British now controlled South Carolina completely.

That night, hiding in a swamp with other survivors, I listened to men making excuses. "We hadn't eaten. We were tired. We had no bayonets."

All true, but the real truth was simpler: we weren't soldiers. Not really. We were citizens playing at war, and when faced with real soldiers, we broke.

An old man joined our group, a Continental veteran of Valley Forge. We offered him some of our foraged food.

"Don't blame yourselves too much," he said quietly. "I ran at my first battle too. The difference is, we learned. We trained. We became soldiers."

"But how?" someone asked. "After this disaster, how do we come back?"

The veteran smiled grimly. "The same way we came back after Long Island, after Brandywine, after every defeat. We learn. We adapt. And we keep fighting."

Looking back now, I understand better. Camden wasn't just a defeat—it was a lesson. Courage alone isn't enough. Numbers alone aren't enough. War is a matter of training, discipline, leadership. Gates forgot that. We militia never knew it.

They say General Greene is coming to take command in the South. They say he'll build a real army, teach us to be real soldiers. After Camden, we know we need it.

I'll join him if he'll have me. Not as militia this time, but as a Continental recruit. Because the shame of running can only be erased one way—by learning to stand.

The British think Camden broke us. Instead, it taught us. Next time, we'll be ready. Next time, we'll be soldiers.

But the memory of that steel wall of bayonets, and the sound of running feet, will haunt me forever.

Chapter 60

Not Worth a Continental

Robert Morris and the Financial Crisis, 1780

Philadelphia - December 1780

I, Robert Morris, stare at the pile of Continental currency on my desk. Beautiful paper, ornate designs—and utterly worthless. A soldier's widow brought them in today, thinking to buy bread. I gave her silver from my own purse instead.

"Mr. Morris?" My clerk enters with the day's reports. "General Washington writes urgently from New Jersey. The army needs supplies."

Of course they do. They always do. I pick up one of the Continental bills. When Congress first issued them in 1775, these were as good as gold. Now it takes forty paper dollars to equal one silver coin. No, fifty. Tomorrow, perhaps sixty.

"The soldiers at Morristown are near mutiny," my clerk continues. "Their pay, when they receive it, buys nothing."

I reach for my ledger—the real one, not the official accounts. My personal fortune, built over decades of merchant ventures, is now all that stands between the army and collapse. Congress can print money, but they cannot print value.

A knock at my door. Thomas Willing, my old business partner, enters.

"Robert," he says gravely, "the merchants want an answer. They won't accept any more Continental currency."

"Show them this," I say, pulling out letters from my European contacts. "French loans are coming. Dutch bankers show interest. We just need to hold on."

But for how long? I've watched this disaster unfold for years. Congress printing more money, prices spiraling upward, faith in our currency collapsing. A dozen eggs that cost one Continental dollar in 1775 now costs forty.

"We need a national bank," I tell Willing. "A real financial system. But try explaining that to thirteen states who can't agree on anything except that they don't want a strong central authority."

I pick up Washington's letter again. Between the lines, I read desperation. The army that survived Valley Forge might yet dissolve over empty purses and worthless pay.

"Send word to my agents," I instruct my clerk. "Have them buy supplies on my personal credit. Send them to Morristown."

"Sir," he protests, "your exposure is already enormous."

Indeed it is. I've pledged my fortune to this cause, used my good name to borrow money, sold my ships and cargoes to feed the army. If we lose this war, I'll be ruined. If we win...well, a beggar in a free nation is still free.

Another messenger arrives—more bad news. Rhode Island refuses to pay its share of war expenses. Virginia declares Continental currency no longer legal tender. In Massachusetts, it takes $100 in paper to buy a pound of tea.

I reach for paper, begin drafting another appeal to the state governors:

"Gentlemen, the fate of our cause rests not only on our armies' valor but on our ability to sustain them. A soldier cannot fight on promises alone..."

Will they listen? They haven't before. Each state guards its own purse, prints its own money, sees itself as sovereign. They don't understand—or refuse to understand—that thirteen weak currencies make one worthless one.

Evening finds me still at my desk. My wife Mary brings dinner, worry etched on her face. She's watched me drain our resources into this bottomless pit of war debt.

"Perhaps," she suggests gently, "it's time to let others carry this burden."

But who would? Who else has both the resources and the foolhardy determination to prop up a failing currency?

I show her Washington's letter. "If the army disperses, all is lost. Not just the war, but the dream of what we could become."

A united nation, strong enough to stand among European powers. A real financial system, backed by more than promises. A future worth building, worth sacrificing for.

I turn back to my accounts, looking for assets yet unsold, credit yet untapped. Tomorrow I'll meet with the Pennsylvania Assembly, beg them again to tax their citizens rather than print more worthless money. Next week I'll press Congress to give me more authority as Superintendent of Finance—authority they're reluctant to grant but desperate to benefit from.

"Not worth a Continental," people say now, laughing at our paper money.

But I, Robert Morris, still believe. Not in the currency—that's beyond saving. But in what it represents: our first fumbling attempts to build a nation. We must learn from this failure, build something better.

If we survive.

I pick up my quill and begin another letter to another reluctant state governor. The army must be fed. The war must be funded. The nation must endure.

Even if it costs me everything I own.

Chapter 61

The Lion and the Fox

Lafayette's Virginia Campaign, 1781

Virginia - Summer 1781

I, Marie-Joseph Paul Yves Roch Gilbert du Motier, Marquis de Lafayette, study the map before me, tracking Cornwallis's movements. Four years ago, I was a naive young nobleman playing at revolution. Now, at twenty-three, I command the defense of Virginia.

"Cornwallis moves north again, sir," my aide reports. "He seems determined to catch us."

I smile. Let him try. These months of maneuvering have taught me patience. "The old lion hunts us," I tell my officers, "but we are the fox, always just out of reach."

How far I've come from that eager boy who first met General Washington! I had to prove myself then—young, foreign, unable to even speak proper English. Now I guard the largest of the original colonies with a mixed force of Continentals and militia.

"Send word to our scouts," I order. "I want to know every move Cornwallis makes. And tell the militia to fire three shots if they spot British foraging parties."

My orders flow more easily in English now. America has changed me, taught me. Valley Forge showed me how to endure. Four years of war taught me strategy. And Washington...mon général, my second father, taught me leadership.

A messenger arrives with a letter from Washington. I break the seal eagerly, scanning his familiar handwriting. He approves my tactics—avoid direct battle, preserve my force, harass the enemy. "You are doing exactly what is necessary," he writes. "Keep Cornwallis occupied."

I fold the letter carefully. Washington sees the larger picture—French forces gathering in the north, the possibility of trapping Cornwallis. My job is to be the bait, to convince the British lion to keep chasing this French fox.

"General!" A rider gallops up. "British cavalry, approaching from the south!"

"Break camp," I order calmly. "We move north, but slowly. Let them think they almost have us."

As we march, I think of Cornwallis—the experienced British commander pursuing this young Frenchman across Virginia. Does he guess he's following a trail I want him to follow? Does he suspect that his pursuit is leading him into a trap?

We skirmish at Richmond, at Malvern Hill, at Green Spring. Each time, I give him a taste of battle, then slip away. My Virginia militia melt into the countryside, only to reappear and strike at his supply lines. We are everywhere and nowhere.

"Your strategy frustrates the men," my aide admits one evening. "They want to fight."

"As did I, when I first arrived," I tell him. "But I have learned that sometimes victory comes not from fighting, but from choosing when not to fight."

June becomes July. The summer heat is oppressive, unlike anything in France. But we persist. Cornwallis pushes toward the coast, toward Yorktown peninsula. Exactly where we want him.

"You're becoming more American than French," one of my officers jokes as I share salt pork and cornbread with the men.

Perhaps I am. I fight for France's interests, yes, but also for something more. This new nation has given me purpose, friendship, a cause worth serving. The idol of my youth - glory - has been replaced by something greater: liberty.

In early August, I write to Washington: "The old lion nears his cage. Yorktown awaits."

As I seal the letter, I remember that young marquis who arrived four years ago, expecting a brief adventure. How little I knew! America has made me a soldier, a leader, a man. Washington has become the father I never had. And this war for liberty has become my own.

"General?" My aide interrupts my reflection. "Cornwallis's army is moving toward Yorktown."

I nod, allowing myself a small smile. The fox has led the lion exactly where he needed to go. Soon Washington will arrive from the north, the French fleet will seal the bay, and the trap will spring shut.

But tonight, as I walk among my men, I think not of strategy but of transformation. The revolution has reshaped us all—this young French aristocrat, these American farmers and merchants, this new nation itself.

Tomorrow we shadow Cornwallis again, maintaining the illusion of the chase. But the hunter, though he doesn't know it yet, is about to become the hunted.

The war's final act approaches. And I, Lafayette, once a boy seeking glory, will help write its ending.

For France. For America. For liberty.

Chapter 62

The World Turned Upside Down

Yorktown, Oct. 1781

Yorktown, Virginia - October 1781

I, George Washington, stand atop our siege works, studying the British positions through my spyglass. Cornwallis is trapped—French ships control the bay, our forces control the land. After six long years, we have them.

"The parallel trenches are complete, Your Excellency," General Knox reports. "Our batteries are ready."

I nod, remembering other sieges, other battles. How far we've come from that untrained army I first commanded at Boston! The men digging those trenches are no longer merely brave patriots—they are professional soldiers, hardened by Valley Forge, trained by von Steuben, tested by years of war.

Lafayette approaches, his face glowing with pride. "Mon général, the French batteries await your order."

I smile at my young friend, remembering the eager boy who arrived four years ago, seeking glory. Now he stands here a proven commander, having masterfully maneuvered Cornwallis into this trap.

"Very well," I say. "At my signal."

I raise my arm. A moment of perfect silence descends.

Then... "FIRE!"

The night erupts in thunder. French and American batteries open up together, the sound magnificent and terrible. Six years of struggle, of retreat and advance, of victory and defeat, have led to this moment.

As the bombardment continues, my mind drifts to earlier days. That Christmas night crossing the Delaware. The desperate winter at Valley Forge. The arrival of the French alliance. Each step, each sacrifice, each triumph and disaster, forming links in a chain that led here.

"General Washington!" A rider approaches. "British counter-battery fire is slackening."

Of course it is. Their gunners face veterans now, not the un-trained militia of Bunker Hill. My army has learned the art of war, paid for those lessons in blood and hardship.

I make my rounds of the siege lines. Here are Rhode Island men who stood with me at Long Island. Here Massachusetts troops who survived Valley Forge. Here Virginians who fought at Mon-mouth. And here, French troops in their pristine uniforms, fight-ing alongside us as brothers.

"Your Excellency." Rochambeau joins me at the observation point. "Cornwallis attempts a breakout across the river."

I almost hope he succeeds. Almost. But our positions are too strong, our troops too well-placed. The British boats, trying to cross to Gloucester Point, are driven back by a storm.

Even nature, it seems, has joined our cause.

Days pass. Our trenches creep closer. The bombardment con-tinues. I watch through my spyglass as Cornwallis's defenses crumble. The mighty British Army, which chased us from New York, which pursued us across New Jersey, which captured Philadelphia, is being systematically destroyed.

On October 17th, a British drummer appears, followed by an officer with a white flag.

Negotiations begin. I insist on the same terms Cornwallis gave at Charleston—the British must march out with colors cased, playing an English tune. They choose "The World Turned Upside Down." How fitting.

As I prepare for the surrender ceremony, I think of all those who didn't live to see this day. The frozen dead at Valley Forge. The boys who fell at Brooklyn Heights. The countless sacrifices that purchased this moment.

The surrender itself passes in a blur of ceremony. Cornwallis, claiming illness, sends his sword by General O'Hara. I direct him to present it to General Lincoln, who had to surrender Charleston. These small symmetries matter.

The British troops march out between lines of French and American soldiers. Their drums beat that telling tune: "The World Turned Upside Down."

Indeed it has. A nation of farmers and merchants has defeated the mightiest empire on Earth. Colonial militia have become a professional army. And I...I have seen a dream of liberty transform into a reality of independence.

Later, in my tent, I write in my diary: "Nothing could exceed the joy of the allied troops on this occasion." But my own joy is tempered by the knowledge that our work is not yet complete.

We have won our independence with French blood and American courage. Now comes the harder task—forging these states into a nation that deserves the sacrifices made to birth it.

Lafayette enters, his young face shining. "It is done, mon général!"

"The war is done, my dear Marquis," I correct him gently. "Our work is just beginning."

But for tonight, let the men celebrate. Let them sing and dance and glory in their triumph. They have earned this moment. They have turned the world upside down.

And I, George Washington, who has carried the weight of this war for six long years, allow myself a moment of quiet satisfaction. We set out to secure our independence. Against all odds, we have succeeded.

Now we must prove ourselves worthy of it.

Post-Revolution

Chapter 63

The Price of Glory

Benedict Arnold

Somewhere in London - December 1781

I, Benedict Arnold, once the most celebrated general in the Continental Army, now sit in London exile, penning these words by candlelight. They call me traitor. Let them. But first, let them hear my tale.

Do they remember Quebec? The wilderness march through Maine, men dying of starvation, yet we pressed on. My leg shattered at Saratoga, yet I led the charge that broke Burgoyne's army. Where was my reward? Congress promoted others—men who had fled while I fought.

The ledger before me shows my debts from serving the cause. Thousands spent from my own purse to supply troops Congress wouldn't feed or clothe. "Submit your accounts," they said, then buried them in committees. Meanwhile, that preening peacock Gates took credit for my victory at Saratoga.

Philadelphia's command should have been my reward. Instead, it became my undoing. They accused me of profiteering—me, who had spent my fortune on their revolution! The court-martial cleared me, but the stain remained. Washington offered words of support but no real aid. He too was a slave to Congress's whims.

And what of my new wife, Peggy? The whispers about her Loyalist family, the social snubs, the petty humiliations. She who had married a hero found herself wed to a man increasingly scorned by his own side.

West Point's command was the final insult. A backwater post for the army's finest field commander. Yet it offered...opportunities. When the British made contact through Peggy's friend, Major André, I told myself I was merely exploring options. But the numbers they offered—£20,000 and a general's commission—would erase my debts and restore my honor.

Honor. I laugh bitterly at the word now. What honor did Congress show when they promoted incompetents over me? What honor was there in leaving soldiers unpaid while politicians grew fat on war contracts?

The plan was perfect. West Point would fall, the Hudson would be severed, the revolution would collapse. A quick end to a war that had lost its way. I would be hailed as a peacemaker, not a traitor.

But André was caught. My encrypted messages discovered. I barely escaped to the British lines as Washington himself arrived at West Point. They hanged André—gallant, cultured André—while I lived. Another burden for my conscience.

Now I sit in London, wearing the red coat I once fought against. The King's supporters toast me in public but whisper behind my back. My own son serves in their army—perhaps he at least will find the glory I sought.

They say I betrayed my country. But what country? We were British subjects who took up arms against our legitimate king. When does rebellion become treason, and treason rebellion? Ask the men who once cheered my charges if they never doubted, never counted the cost.

Washington. His name torments me still. He alone seemed to understand my worth, yet even he couldn't shield me from Congress's pettiness. I hear he crushed Cornwallis at Yorktown using the very tactics I pioneered at Saratoga. At least my lessons served someone well.

Peggy calls me to bed, but sleep brings no peace. In my dreams, I'm back at Saratoga, leading the charge that made America believe it could win. I feel again the bullet shatter my leg—the same leg that had been wounded at Quebec. Glory and pain, forever intertwined.

History will call me traitor, I know. They will forget Quebec, forget Valcour Island, forget Saratoga. They will remember only West Point and André. So be it. But let them remember also that Benedict Arnold was once the revolution's brightest sword, its most audacious commander.

Let them remember that I gave America victories when it needed them most. And if I finally took payment for my service from the other side—well, every man has his price. Mine was being denied the glory I had earned with my blood.

I am Benedict Arnold. Hero and traitor, patriot and turncoat. Let history judge me as it will. I have learned that glory, like liberty, comes with a price. I merely chose to accept a different payment.

Chapter 64

The Price of Loyalty

New York City - November 1782

The early winter wind whips across the harbor as I, Thomas Bradford, former merchant of Boston, now refugee in New York, watch another wave of ships depart for Nova Scotia. Tomorrow, we join the exodus.

"Father?" My daughter Anne's voice draws me from my thoughts. "Mr. Harrison says we can only take two trunks per person. How do we pack a lifetime into two trunks?"

How indeed? Twenty-five years of building a business, a reputation, a life—all to be abandoned or sold for pennies because we chose the wrong side.

"Your mother's china," I tell her. "Your grandmother's silver. The family Bible. Pack what can't be replaced."

Sarah, my wife, sits at her writing desk, penning one last letter to her sister Mary, who chose the patriot cause. They haven't spoken in six years. Will they ever again?

"Perhaps we could stay," Sarah suggests softly, not for the first time. "Others are taking the oath to the new government."

I shake my head. "They'll never trust us. Remember what happened to the Wilsons? Tar and feathers, their home burned. No, we've made our choice. Now we must live with it."

The house is a chaos of packing and farewells. Our son James, sixteen, argues to take his father's medical books—he dreams of studying medicine in London. Little William, only ten, clutches his toy soldier wearing a red coat—a gift from happier days.

"Mr. Bradford?" Our former clerk, David, appears at the door. Though he sided with the rebels, he's remained decent to us. "I've found a buyer for the warehouse. He'll give forty percent of value."

Forty percent. Six months ago, we might have held out for more. But with the flood of properties being sold by departing Loyalists, we must take what we can get.

"Tell him yes," I say. What choice do we have?

That evening, our last in the house, old friends gather—those who haven't already sailed or chosen to stay under the new republic. The Harrisons, the Wentworths, the Cabots—names that once meant something in Boston society.

"To England," someone toasts.

"To Nova Scotia," adds another.

"To loyalty," says old Mrs. Cabot, her voice bitter. Her son died fighting for the king.

Later, after the guests leave, I find Sarah crying over her mother's portrait—too large to take.

"Leave it," I tell her gently. "Perhaps someday, when tempers cool, we'll return. Or our children will."

But we both know it's a lie. America - our America - is gone.

Morning brings a flurry of last-minute decisions. What to take? What to leave? Every object holds memories, represents choices made and paths taken.

The harbor is crowded with ships preparing to sail. British authorities try to maintain order among the flood of refugees. I see familiar faces everywhere—merchants, craftsmen, clergy who stayed loyal to the Crown. Now we're all equal in exile.

"They'll call us traitors in their histories," Harrison mutters beside me as we wait to board.

"No," I correct him. "They won't mention us at all. Victors write the histories, and we're merely an inconvenient footnote."

As we finally board our ship, I watch my children's faces. James tries to be brave, but I see his fear. Anne can't stop crying. Only little William seems excited, treating it as an adventure.

"Look, Father!" he calls out, pointing to the British flag snapping in the wind. "We're sailing to England!"

I put my arm around Sarah as New York recedes. Behind us lies everything we built, everything we loved. Ahead lies...what? Nova Scotia's harsh winters? London's crowded streets? How does one start over at fifty?

The ship clears the harbor. Sarah grips my hand.

"We did what we thought was right," she whispers.

"Yes." But was being right worth the cost?

I think of Mary's last letter to Sarah: "Sister, there need not be bitterness between us. We each chose according to our conscience."

Our conscience. Our loyalty. Our choice.

As America fades into the distance, I wonder how many others are paying the price of conscience today. How many other families are being torn apart, how many other lives disrupted, because they chose the losing side in this revolution?

They call it independence. For us, it's exile.

For king and conscience, we're leaving our home, becoming strangers in a land we've never seen. Behind us lies a new nation, born in rebellion. Ahead lies an uncertain future.

God save the king.

God help us all.

Chapter 65

Three Americans in Paris

Paris - Evening of September 3, 1783

The private dining room at Café de la Paix glowed with candle-light as I, Benjamin Franklin, watched my fellow commissioners settle into their chairs. John Adams, ever proper even in relaxation, adjusted his napkin methodically. John Jay, looking younger than his years despite the strain of negotiations, signaled for wine.

"Well, gentlemen," I offered, raising my glass, "we have this day signed away His Majesty's thirteen colonies."

"Not signed away, Dr. Franklin," Adams corrected quickly. "Secured their independence. There's a difference."

"So there is," I smiled. "Though I suspect King George sees it otherwise."

The waiter brought a bottle of fine Bordeaux. Jay examined the label appreciatively. "A 1762. Pre-war vintage. How appropriate."

"To independence," I proposed.

"To the United States of America," Adams added.

"To peace," Jay concluded.

We drank, letting the moment settle around us. Outside, Paris continued its evening bustle, unaware that history had been made this day. Inside, three tired Americans contemplated the magnitude of what we'd achieved.

"Do you remember," I asked, "when this all seemed impossible? When independence was just a dream that might cost us our necks?"

Adams snorted. "I remember suggesting independence in Congress and being looked at as though I'd proposed flying to the moon."

"Yet here we sit," Jay mused, "commissioners of a free and independent nation, treating as equals with the greatest powers of Europe."

The first course arrived—soup for Adams and Jay, while I chose oysters. Some habits of Philadelphia couldn't be broken, even in Paris.

"Tell me, Franklin," Adams leaned forward, "when did you first believe it was possible? Really possible?"

I considered the question. "Perhaps at Saratoga. When word reached Paris that Burgoyne had surrendered, I knew we had a real chance. The French knew it too."

"Saratoga," Jay nodded. "Gates's great victory, though Arnold did the fighting."

"Poor Benedict," I sighed. "Such promise, such waste."

"Damn him," Adams said firmly. "His treason nearly cost us everything."

"Yet we survived it," I pointed out. "As we survived all the dark moments. The retreat from New York. Valley Forge. Camden."

"Washington," Jay said quietly. "We survived because of Washington."

We paused, thinking of our commander-in-chief. Even now, he kept the army together, ensuring peace would stick.

"Have you read his latest dispatch?" Adams asked. "He worries about the army. About paying them, about their future."

"He worries about everything," I said. "That's what made him the right man. He carries the burden of the future on his shoulders."

The main course arrived—duck for Adams, beef for Jay, fish for myself. The wine flowed freely now, loosening tongues and memories.

"What do you think, gentlemen?" Jay asked. "Will this republic of ours survive?"

"It must," Adams replied firmly. "We've staked everything on it."

"If," I raised a cautionary finger, "we can keep it. A republic requires virtue, gentlemen. Constant virtue."

"And constant vigilance," Jay added. "Britain will not easily forget this defeat. They'll look for weakness, for division among us."

"Let them look," Adams declared. "We're not thirteen colonies anymore. We're one nation."

"Are we?" I asked softly. "New York and Virginia? Massachusetts and Georgia? Can such different places truly remain united?"

Silence fell as we contemplated this. The waiter cleared our plates, brought cheese and port.

"The Constitution," Jay said finally. "That's our next battle. The Articles of Confederation aren't enough. We need a stronger union."

"Careful," Adams warned. "Too strong a government and we'll have merely exchanged one tyranny for another."

"Too weak," I countered, "and we'll fall apart. Balance, gentlemen. We must find balance."

The conversation turned to specifics—boundaries secured in the treaty, fishing rights, debts to be paid. But underlying it all was the larger question: what would this new nation become?

"You know," I said, gesturing with my port glass, "I've been thinking about that moment in Philadelphia, when we signed the Declaration. Do you remember how hot it was?"

"How could I forget?" Adams smiled. "You kept insisting we close the windows because of the flies."

"And Franklin made his famous quip about the sun carved on Washington's chair," Jay added.

"A rising sun or a setting sun," I remembered. "Now we know. A rising sun indeed."

"But will it keep rising?" Adams persisted. "This experiment in self-government—it's never been tried on this scale before."

"That's what makes it glorious," I said. "We're not just securing independence for ourselves, but offering hope to all humanity. If we succeed..."

"If we succeed," Jay finished, "we change the world."

The candles had burned low. Outside, Paris had grown quiet. Three Americans sat in a French café, contemplating a future they had helped create but would not fully see.

"Gentlemen," Adams raised his glass one final time, "to the future United States of America. May we be worthy of what we've started here."

"To the future," Jay and I echoed.

We drank the toast, each lost in our own thoughts. I looked at my fellow commissioners—Adams, the passionate advocate; Jay, the thoughtful diplomat; myself, the old philosopher. We had done what we could. Now it would be up to others to carry it forward.

As we prepared to leave, I found myself thinking of that long-ago summer in Philadelphia. How young we all were, how certain of our cause. Now, older and perhaps wiser, we had achieved what we'd dreamed of then.

"One last thing," I said at the door. "History will want to know about this day. What shall we tell them?"

Adams straightened his coat. "Tell them we did our duty."

Jay smiled. "Tell them we secured their future."

"No," I said, "let's tell them the truth. We gave them a republic—if they can keep it."

We stepped out into the Paris night, three Americans who had helped birth a nation. Behind us lay years of war and sacrifice. Ahead lay an uncertain but promising future.

The experiment would continue. The dream would be tested. But here, on this September evening in Paris, we had given it its chance.

The rest would be up to posterity.

Also by Barry Robbins

About the author

Barry hails from Philadelphia and built a career with a prominent international accounting firm, taking him to New York, Washington, D.C., and San Francisco before a new chapter brought him to Finland. He and his Finnish wife adopted two daughters from China, and their family lived in Helsinki for twelve years before he returned to the U.S., now calling Florida home.

Barry's literary work blends satire, history, and whimsy. Known for his Trump satires, including "The Weave", he's earned three gold medals for his sharp wit. His curiosity also led to "Lessons from the Sidewalk", a playful journey where historical icons mingle with everyday items, and "Dostoevsky's Borscht", an inventive mashup of history, culture, and cuisine.

Barry's most recent works reveal a thoughtful turn: "Tears of the Titans" examines the regrets of historical icons, while "Voices of the Civil War" and "Voices of the American Revolution" bring an immersive, personal lens to these tumultuous periods. With a knack for balancing wit and insight, Barry's writing invites readers to explore history from new, intimate perspectives.